✝ THE E....

A Novel

CÉSAR VIDAL

Original title: *El exiliado*

The Agustin Agency is a division of The Agustin Agency Services, LLC, and is a registered trademark. www.theagustinagency.com

This book can be ordered in high volume as gifts, for fundraising events or for ministry or business training by writing to Sales@TheAgustinAgency.com.

For wholesale sales to bookstores, distributors or to resell, please contact the distributor Anchor Distributors at 1-800-444-4484.

Scripture quotations marked NKJV are from the New King James Version of the Bible, public domain.

Translation: Editorial Renuevo
Translation Adaptation: Kadi Kool
Proofread: TLM Editorial Services, Inc.
Interior Design: Deditorial
Cover Design: Chris Ward

ISBN: 978-1-950604-142 (Paper)
ISBN: 978-1-950604-20-3 (E-book)

Printed in the United States of America.

20 21 22 23 BETHANY PRESS 9 8 7 6 5 4 3 2 1

contents

PREFACE

When I wrote *The Exile,* I had in mind the exiles who have been and who will unfortunately continue to be among us throughout human history, in all ages and for all kinds of reasons. This is precisely why the protagonist remains anonymous throughout the book; he could have been any of the millions of people who have been forced to leave the land of their birth and go into exile to avoid prison, ruin, torture, and even death.

The protagonist flees from a sixteenth-century Spain that is in the grips of terror instilled by the Holy Inquisition. As early as 1518, the Courts of Castile had petitioned King Carlos I for the Inquisition to become a court where, yes, torture continued to be used, but with restraint and where, the new arts of torment that the inquisitors so reveled in would be excluded. Those representatives of the people also requested that prisoners be informed of the charges against them, that they be allowed to have lawyers, and that they not be held in underground prisons with no light. They pleaded for these terms to be accepted because many innocent people were being convicted. Many were also leaving the kingdom and this brought with it economic losses. The court procurators certainly were not asking for tolerance, much less freedom of conscience, but they did ask that an institution that committed horrific acts, sowing death and panic throughout the society, be tempered. Nevertheless, the Grand Inquisitor refused to grant a single one of the petitions, knowing that, as stated in inquisitors' manuals, the fundamental purpose of the institution was *ut metuant*, that is, to create fear. If the totalitarian brutality, the ability to end lives and estates, and the power to perpetuate the curse on future generations were even minimally relaxed, the institution would not be able to maintain the iron hand with which it controlled the kingdoms of the Spanish monarchy.

Because of all these circumstances, I placed my exile in Inquisition-era Spain as a reflection of so many others who lived in other ages, places, and circumstances. I also did so because on his way to freedom, the exile was living through a momentous historical event. The West was dividing into countries that embraced the Reformation and returned to the principles found in the Bible and those that remained faithful to Rome and to an absolutist worldview of dogmatic truths imposed from above. These circumstances have not lost their relevance in a world that is shaken by fear, paralyzed by epidemics, a world that struggles to shake off yokes of injustice and, not infrequently, wanders aimlessly, not knowing where to go.

In no small measure, our world, like that of *The Exile*, is still divided between those who seek freedom and those who prefer to be subjugated; between those who, if need be, go into exile and those who pursue exiles, even abroad; between those who are in favor of everything remaining the same even if it is evil, and those who harbor a hope in their heart for a better tomorrow. This is what this novel is about. And now I will not keep you any longer from your reading.

Miami, Spring 2020

CHAPTER I

The exile held his breath. Or rather, it was as if his breath held him. As if all of a sudden, he harbored doubts and his plan no longer seemed sound. As if he found himself on the edge of a dark abyss and were afraid to jump across.

But that only lasted a moment—a fleeting moment. He slowly expelled the air that had been trapped in his lungs and crouched down. He had thought it through countless times, and just as he had planned and rehearsed it, with his body hunched, almost completely bent over, he slipped forward under the cover of the shadowy gray dusk. He knew he had enough time to cross the empty corral, jump over the low stone wall like an almost soundless exhale, and blend his own narrow shadow with the thick ones cast by the forest trees.

Only a few more steps and the deep evening darkness, which came just in time, would shield him as if it were a well-woven cloak ready to provide comforting shelter during a storm. Indeed, the exile felt that the heavy darkness falling through the branches of the trees embraced him warmly. He hastened on, with a sense that he was able to control the multitude of sounds in the dense forest. He walked carefully, trying to step so that no fallen twig or pile of leaves would give him away.

He knew without any doubt whatsoever that everything hinged on him going unnoticed. Not only in town, not only in the region, not only in the kingdom, but across the rest of Europe, until he reached the city of refuge to which thousands were fleeing for safety and protection.

At least until leaving the kingdom, the exile would need to travel at night and sleep during the day in places where no one could find him. For now, he was sure he could count on a few hours' head start. Surely his escape would go unnoticed until noon the next day, or perhaps even a bit later.

He had bolted the door of his room from the inside and then had gone out through the window, being careful to close it by pulling a little string attached to the inside. Yes, the thought that he was either asleep or ill would delay their noticing his absence. Unless of course…

The unexpected murmur of the nearby brook startled the exile from his until-then unbroken flow of thoughts. He hurried towards the bridge that spanned the meandering stream. The structure, made of flimsy wood, stood exposed in the moonlight, but if he hurried he would only be visible for a few moments to any unwelcome gaze.

He must have been twenty paces away from it when his ears detected a sound. At first it was a long way off, barely discernible except for the silence of the night. Then he felt a slight tremor through the soles of his boots. Horses! Yes, they were horses. And more than one.

He ran towards the bridge trying not to make any noise. He reached it in no time and then looked for a way down to the riverbed. In another circumstance, he would have taken the trouble to find the best way to get down without stumbling or getting wet. Unfortunately, he didn't have time for that now.

He dashed to the right side and began to clamber down under the bridge, trying not to slip or trip. He felt with displeasure how water from the stream began to soak through his boots, first the soles of his feet, then his ankles ... an extremely unpleasant sensation because the water was icy cold. He would be lucky if he didn't catch pneumonia. But now was not the time to analyze the effects of the icy dampness that was numbing his toes.

He had barely managed to reach the other side where the bridge met the road, when he felt a powerful, deafening, thunderous rumble approaching at full speed. Soon the mighty clatter of horses' hooves passed over his head.

Amid the deafening roar, the exile tried to ascertain how many horses there were. Two at least, maybe three or even more. However many there were, who could they be carrying? One or two Familiars of the Holy Office, for sure. As a rule, they didn't like to travel alone. One or two more ... maybe someone from town. Maybe ... maybe even ... his brother. Of course, he couldn't be sure. No, he could not, but it wasn't impossible either. Of course, it would not be the first time that a person betrayed or even killed a relative to satisfy the ravenous appetite of that peculiar institution.

The exile waited until the sound of furious galloping died away and then emerged for a moment from underneath the bridge. Cautiously but quickly he took off his boots, turning them upside down to empty out the water that had seeped in, and took off his stockings, wringing them as if he were drying laundry.

Though not what he had planned, he would have to interrupt his flight and rest in that part of the forest, taking advantage of the almost total darkness that it afforded him. In an attempt to calm down, he told himself that this might not be so bad after all. For some time—perhaps even days—they would think they were hot on his heels when, in fact, he would be trailing behind them. It was not the time to be happy at all, but he couldn't help but smile. He even had to work hard to keep from laughing out loud. God was indeed very good, and not only because the psalmist said so.

CHAPTER 2

The exile may have wanted to rest, but this objective proved to be beyond the realm of possibility. Every time he was about to fall into a deep sleep, the smallest noise awakened him with a panicked jolt. Not once had it been horses or human steps, but that fact had not removed one bit of anxiety from his heart.

Finally, after no more than three hours of dozing, he had to face the fact that he would no longer be able to sleep. He found that his boots were still damp and that his stockings were still wet. He certainly didn't like it, but he had no choice but to accept his circumstances. He would have to wait a whole day without being able to continue. A whole day lost.

The exile took a deep breath. He was aware that he had to leave the region and then the kingdom as soon as possible, and what had just happened did not exactly help towards making that plan a reality. Of course, it was also true that things do not always go as planned. One had only to think about what happened with the plan to have him arrested. Just two days earlier he was preparing his satchel to go into the hills and spend a few days in the scrublands. This was his habit at this time of year.

He was about to leave the house when he heard someone knocking at the door. First, it was a soft sound. Then came a succession of soft but uninterrupted knocks, like tapping. Finally, he heard his name. He recognized the voice immediately and almost before he knew it, he was standing at the door.

"What are you doing here?" he asked in complete surprise.

"Oh, thank God you haven't left the house yet!" exclaimed the woman as she grabbed his hands.

"What's the matter?"

"Come," she answered in a voice filled with anguish. "Sit down, please."

He smiled. What was this all about? What could be so serious that it had frightened his neighbor?

"Sit down, please," she repeated, anxiously.

She had taken him by the hand and practically dragged him to one of the kitchen stools.

"Well?" he asked once he was seated.

"The first thing is not to be frightened," she began. "Don't be frightened, I beg of you."

"I'm not going to be frightened," he said with a smile. "I assure you. What's this all about?"

"The Holy Office is going to investigate you."

He stifled as best he could the horror he felt at these words. They were only a few words, but for an instant he couldn't breathe. It was like an unexpected blow to the chest or a hard kick to the lower abdomen.

"Do you mean they will come to arrest me?" he asked when he could breathe again.

"No ... no ... I think ... well, maybe they just said it to scare you a little. Yes, yes, to scare you, but for nothing else."

He felt a rush of tenderness towards her rise from his heart and lodge in his throat. If they were talking about it, they must have been very sure because it wasn't like them to just frighten.... It was true that the Holy Office's primary goal was based on *ut metuant,* let them fear, but when they investigated, when they arrested, when they interrogated, it was not primarily to frighten people. In fact, it was to imprison them without letting them know the charges against them and subject them to various forms of torture. This was in order to make them confess to something they had not been informed of, and in the end, as targets of anonymous accusations from enemies, to sentence them to an ignominious punishment that would fall upon the whole family and could very well include burning at the stake.

"And what do you think I should do?" he asked the unexpected informant.

"Leave," she replied. It was one word. Just one. Yet life and death hung on that word, as if it were a powerful and magical talisman.

"Are you sure?"

She did not reply. She just nodded. It was a quiet gesture, but the way she did it left no room for doubt.

"Now?"

The woman nodded again, her eyes swimming with tears. She managed to keep them from overflowing, but suddenly, unexpectedly, a single, sparkling tear rolled down her right cheek. There it remained, suspended between heaven and earth, her pupil and the ground. As if it didn't know where to go, as if it were afraid of its destiny and aware of the abyss that stretched before it. The man was surprised to think that the tear was like him, immobilized, but at the same time in need of escaping his place of origin.

"Thank you," he said as he took her hands in his, "from the bottom of my heart. You have saved my life."

The woman shook her head as the tear slid down to the collar of her white blouse and into her garment.

"No. You have saved mine. Twice."

He felt a lump form in his throat at these words.

"I will always be in your debt," she said. "Now you must leave."

The woman nodded her head. Maybe she wanted to say something more, hug him, even kiss him, but she merely turned abruptly and, reaching the door to the street, left at a run.

He did not waste a single moment. He looked for the largest shoulder bags he had and put in two changes of clothing. Then he packed as much food as he thought he would need to make it to the border of the kingdom. The blanket could be tied to the outside ... then ... those two books ... yes, those two books were indispensable ... the instruments of his profession ... and something to cover his head. The cloak, of course the cloak. Yes, that was all.

He spent the next few hours planning how he would leave the house undetected that night. Then he sat with the bags resting on his knees and stared as the sun crept lazily towards the horizon, waiting several hours until the first shadows fell. Then he was on his way.

Only at one point as he left the town did he look back. It was when he reached a low hill where he could see everything. For a few moments, he watched as the first rays of the moon struck the rustic tower of the church with silver light, as the dusky shadows crept bit by bit over the town square, and as lights came on in some of the houses. Then, as if conjured by a prodigious magician, images from other places in the kingdom appeared before his eyes. He recalled proud cathedrals and secluded cloisters, dormant universities and fertile fields, snow-capped mountains and bustling ports.

All of this and much more came to his mind in dozens of memories, like the ceaseless waves that crash onto an immovable coastline, only to retreat feeble and frayed. He blinked and fixed his eyes on everything that lay before him as if to engrave the place on his heart, and then turned away. He didn't dare look back again, even once. He quickened his pace in order to leave the kingdom as soon as possible.

CHAPTER 3

That day, while hiding under the bridge and waiting for his clothes to dry, the exile had plenty of time to reflect. He was aware that if he did manage to escape from the kingdom—and he was going to do it, yes, with God's help he had to—his life would not begin at zero but below zero. A great deal below zero. In other words, he, and he was not rich, would now be less than a beggar. However, despite his total loss of fortune, he still had to eat, clothe himself, and find lodging.

He was in this plight because his country was the way it was. Yes, but why was his country like this? The exile thought that perhaps it was due to centuries of allowing someone else to think for its people. Clergymen, nobles, kings, and the privileged decided what was good and what was bad, what was allowed and what was prohibited, what should be believed and what should be rejected, what should be done and what was not lawful to do.

In the kingdom he was now leaving, there was nothing to fear if one were only a sheep. Well, also if in addition not a drop of Jewish, Moorish, Black, or Indian blood flowed through one's veins. Because if one's blood was not what was considered pure ... it was a sure way to end up burned at the stake.

But the rest, as long as they bleated with the proper sound and went down the paths and lanes designated by the clergymen and nobles, as long as they did not stray from the established cattle road, they would be more or less safe.

The real problem arose when someone decided to be a salmon. Yes, a salmon, which as anyone knows swims against the current to ensure its survival and that of its species. If anyone decided to be a salmon, even if the vast majority didn't know it, the outcome could be fatal. Not attending every single religious festival, not nodding in agreement with all of the idiotic things a priest might utter from the pulpit with impunity, not spitting hatred against the Moors, who had disappeared from the land centuries ago, or against the Jews of whom not a trace remained, would be reason enough to arouse suspicion.

Also suspect was not working on Saturday, not eating pork, changing one's clothes on the weekend, or simply ... reading. Why learn to read if the prayers that lead us to heaven can be memorized without having to understand a single word? Why educate oneself beyond learning how to raise sheep or till the soil? Why know anything more than absolute submission to those who live off the sweat and blood of people who toiled, worked, and built? Why?

For the exile, the answer was obvious. At the very least, so as not to become a two-legged beast that differed from a four-legged one in something more than merely being able to poorly articulate a few words.

To learn, to know, to discover something that goes beyond knowing where the threshing grounds, the stream, or the town church are located; to let the mind soar like birds that migrate in the winter, and after traveling to unknown places, return in the spring; to truly discover why we are here and understand that it isn't just to pay taxes to unscrupulous authorities or hand over tithes to greedy clergymen ... yes, the exile had longed for all of that for a very long time.

When he returned from the university, he had not worked in the olive groves and vineyards as others did. Nor had he desired gold and glory or crossed the seas in their pursuit. Even less had he wanted to end up in an office like one of the clerks, judges, or accountants who abounded in the kingdom. The exile, unlike the vast majority of students who passed through the university, had left the classrooms perhaps not believing in his professors, but longing for more, much more knowledge than he had managed to receive up to that point.

Every night by the light of a candle, he had devoted himself to studying, studying that complemented and not infrequently replaced the teaching he had received during his years as a student. The exile had truly cherished those times, which were often lit by another glow, this one coming from daybreak and revealing that he had not slept a wink all night. He never cared in the least, because in those hours stolen from sleep, he had learned.

Yes, he had learned in the noblest sense of the word. The centuries-old, hardened crust of superstition, of neglect and ignorance, of avid fanaticism, that crust, which had accumulated over hundreds of years on the bodies and souls of the subjects of the kingdom, had at first cracked, then broken apart and finally fallen off piece by piece.

In the beginning he was happy. He was like an exhausted galley slave who is told that a royal pardon has set him free, or a terminally ill man who learns from his doctor that a cure has been found, or a famished beggar who receives news that he has inherited a sizeable fortune. A deep joy, an almost blinding light, a clean vision that at times took his breathing away, welled up from the books he was slowly buying. He was happy and, moreover, he knew it.

But later ... later, without question, fear had set in. He couldn't have said exactly when this happened, but he realized one day that he had to watch his words, his steps, even the smallest of his actions. He understood that a misinterpreted comment, a malicious complaint, or an envious neighbor could mean the end of his happiness. When all is said and done, his kind neighbor had not really revealed anything surprising. She had simply confirmed his worst suspicions.

CHAPTER 4

The exile crossed the border of the realm with ease. In reality, it was much easier than he had expected. For several days he had slept hidden during the day and traveled through the night. Not once did he cross paths with his pursuers. He concluded that they must think he was ahead of them, and that in their push to catch up with him, they had only succeeded in moving farther away. As he reflected on this, the exile smiled. He had, after all, been convinced for a long time that everything rested in the hands of God, a very different god from the one worshipped by those who wanted to capture him and take his life.

The exile had run completely out of food and had been walking for almost a day with no other plan than to head north, when most unexpectedly, he noticed a thin wisp of smoke rising up in the distance. He stopped, undecided. It could be coming from a campfire, a wildfire, or from a house.

Finally, he determined that whatever the case it would be worthwhile to go see. He had to trek up and down a couple of hills to get a better view of the situation. He discovered that a jagged chimney embedded in a stone roof was the source of the phenomenon that had caught his eye. In another place and time he might have steered clear of it but now, with no food and no sign of a stream for water anywhere, he had no choice but to approach the house and see if he could get a little food and maybe even a place to spend the night.

He went down the knoll he was standing on and covered the distance to the house, about three hundred paces. He had only a few strides to go when a man emerged from the right side of the building. He had a scythe in his hand, either to sharpen it or to brandish it in warning.

Instinctively, the exile raised his right hand to his heart, bowed his head in respect, and asked if he was the man of the house. The individual frowned and replied, haltingly, as if he were not speaking his mother tongue. The exile thought that the man could be one of the people who came to work in that country for a time, and then after they had saved some money, would return to their country of origin in hopes of living a more comfortable life. The exile supposed that the reception from this man would in all likelihood depend on the treatment the man himself had received in this country.

"I have run out of food," he began, instinctively raising his voice, as if shouting enabled others to better understand a foreign language. "Would you be so kind as to...?"

"I have worrk," the farmer interrupted, "iff you worrk I giff fud."

The exile smiled and agreed with a nod.

"Take axe and chop," said the farmer, pointing in quick succession to an axe leaning against one of the walls of the house and a pile of logs.

The exile put his shoulder bags down and picked up the axe. It was heavy and rough to the touch, the type of tool that is used to chop more than just small branches. Then he walked to the logs and started splitting them. He had only very occasionally performed this task, and as a result soon felt a pain that started in his shoulders and then radiated ever more sharply down his spine until it hit his kidneys; at the same time the pain also spread down his arm to the tips of his fingers.

Initially, it was an uncomfortable pain, but in a very short time, each blow he dealt the wood repaid him with a redoubled stab of pain from his right hand to his waist. Soon, his knuckles, wrist, elbow, and shoulder began to discharge painful waves each time he brought the axe down on the wood. Unexpectedly, he found himself smiling and thinking that it seemed as if the wood were retaliating and hitting him back.

Amid the growing pain in his limbs, he noticed that his heart was beating faster and that the sweat already bathing his entire body began to fall in big, fat drops from his forehead. But what dismayed him most was discovering that blisters were forming on his hands.

For an instant, the exile felt ashamed of himself. He was embarrassed by his physical weakness and the little endurance his body displayed. In fact, in the hours that followed, he believed more than once that he would not be able to keep on without fainting at some point. He looked apprehensively at the pile of wood he had yet to cut when he heard the farmer say:

"Water, therre."

He looked where the man was pointing and saw an old barrel with a ladle hanging from a rope. Trembling with exhaustion he walked over, plunged the dipper through the dark surface, and raising it to his lips, greedily gulped down the water with an urgency he had never felt before. He was indeed beyond exhausted after hours of work. First in his mouth and throat, but then spreading throughout his body, he felt the water refresh and reinvigorate his aching limbs. How good it was and how good God was for having created water!

The sun had begun to set slowly down to the uneven mauve horizon, when the man appeared at the door of the house and said:

"Come."

He was about to enter the dwelling when he received a new order:

"Firrst, wash hands," the man said, gesturing to the right.

He glanced around until he saw a well with a wooden bucket resting on its edge. It was no small effort to walk over to it. His legs threatened to buckle as if they were rags, and the pain gripping his back seemed more acute than ever.

Still, he made it and for a moment he leaned on the rough stone surface, seeking to regain the strength that had been shattered in the previous hours.

He discovered to his dismay that the bucket was empty. The thought of having to throw the bucket to the bottom of the well and then pull it up seemed overwhelming. However, he didn't have a choice. He listened as the bucket hit the surface of the water and then thought he heard it sink, gurgling, to the bottom of the well.

Then he gripped the rope attached to the bucket, and as he did so, he felt the rough hemp rub against his wounds. He pulled, and though admittedly the weight was not much, each time he pulled, it seemed to him that an instrument of torture was venting its rage on the palms of his hands. All of a sudden it occurred to him to put the rope under his arm and pull that way. Only when he saw the bucket appear over the well wall did the exile use his hands again. He should have just washed his hands, but when he felt the cold around his hands, from his fingertips all the way to his wrists, he stopped. He didn't move. He just let himself feel the icy liquid, pleasant and painful at the same time.

"Come," he heard the man say, plucking him from his momentary daydreaming.

The exile quickly washed his hands and headed for the house.

"Come in," the man said as he pushed the door open.

It took a few moments for his eyes to adjust to the gloomy darkness inside the house. In that part of the world ... yes, the room did not have a window, and perhaps it did not have one because one would have to pay a special tax for such a privilege. A despicable idea of the powers that be: to come up with new levies for everything! This farmer probably broke his back from sun-up to sun-down every day, in sunshine, in the rain, and in the cold north wind, but the authorities demanded payment from him if he wanted the sun's rays to enter his house and illuminate it.

They sat down at the table. In the background, a large pot was hanging over a meager fire. Thanks to the light streaming through the half-open door, the exile was able to pick out three more shapes huddled together in the room—a woman who seemed apprehensive and two children, a boy and a girl, who clung to her skirts and looked at him with a mixture of fear and mistrust. Yes, surely in their eyes he was an intruder who came to deprive them of their hard-earned morsel of bread, arduously wrested from the ground. The man spoke to his family and explained who the exile was, and he did so in words that were familiar to the exile. Thank God they spoke a language he knew!

The woman uncovered the pot and a puff of steam billowed up to the ceiling. The smell of the stew was neither pleasant nor appealing, but the exile was faint with hunger and in desperate need of a hot meal in his belly. In fact, when he saw her ladle the stew into his bowl, he felt truly blissful.

He bowed his head and quietly said a prayer as the family made the sign of the cross, and began to eat using the slice of bread he had been given as a spoon. He couldn't tell what exactly he was eating. Neither the texture nor the taste was appetizing, but he was filled with gratitude.

He had swallowed half the bowl when the man in of house grabbed his left hand and turned it around. He looked at his palm, ran his fingers over it and said:

"You ... you no villain."

The exile replied in the language the man had used with his family. He knew enough to communicate fluently.

"You speak my language?" asked the peasant in surprise.

"A little, yes, and you are right, I am not a villain."

"A nobleman?"

"A physician," replied the exile.

"Did you study?"

The exile nodded.

"That's why you have fine, smooth hands that are now filled with blisters," said the man of the house, although it was not clear if he was merely thinking aloud. Silent for a moment, he finally said:

"I have a little wine—would you like to share a jug?"

"That's kind of you but I wouldn't want to..."

The man did not let him continue. Before the exile was able to finish his sentence, his host had risen to his feet, plunged into the thick shadows of the narrow abode, and after some noise of indeterminate origin, placed two earthenware mugs on the table.

"Here's to your health!" he said as he raised his mug in salute, before bringing it to his lips.

The exile repeated the gesture, though he barely moistened his lips.

"It's not good for man like you, a doctor, to ruin your hands. You're not used to it and that's because you're not a farmer... ah, the life of a farmer is very hard, sir, yes it is. God punished our first parents with work, and we have had to bear the brunt of it."

"Work is not a punishment from God," said the exile, and then immediately regretted having let the words out.

The peasant frowned when he heard the exile's statement.

"No?" he said in a voice seeped in doubt. "Is it not? Well, the way we live..."

The exile hesitated. On the one hand, he was convinced that this conversation was veering into dangerous territory; on the other, he was far from his hometown and felt incapable of remaining silent.

"No," he finally said with a sigh, "in the beginning it wasn't like that. God created Adam, placed him in the Garden of Eden and told him to tend and keep it. He commanded him to work and Adam obeyed. All of this happened before his disobedience and banishment from the Garden."

"Did Adam live in paradise as badly as I do?" asked the farmer in disbelief.

"No," replied the exile, "he lived like none of us has ever lived, but he worked. Of course, not like you do every day or like me, today, but he worked."

"So, you're telling me that work is not a punishment from God as the priest says?" asked the surprised peasant.

"No, it's not," replied the exile spurred by the mention of the cleric. "Work was created by God for the common good. The only thing that is bad is the way men have spoiled this plan of God. Working for oneself... or for others, is very good. There is nothing dishonorable about working with your hands. Nothing at all. What is intolerable is that others take advantage of that work; that they take away the fruits of one's toil with taxes; that they use it so that they do not have to work."

The exile noted that the peasant raised his eyebrows and then immediately raised his mug to his mouth, draining its contents with one long swig. It was obvious that the exile's words had confounded him, and he was not able to digest them.

"Is that why," he began to speak at last, "you didn't tell me who you were and just started to chop wood?"

"Chopping wood is as worthy as issuing a verdict, celebrating mass, or governing," replied the exile.

"Your food is going to get cold," the woman intervened, "and it is not good cold."

"Yes," said the exile, who sensed a certain note of alarm in her words. "I think you are right."

CHAPTER 5

The exile stayed with the family for a few days. During his stay, the exile saw that in reality the life of these people was not so bad. Yes, it was true that it was subject to contingencies such as rain and sun, disease and drought, insects and frost. Nevertheless with all that, it was a simple, productive, and to some extent, fortunate life. Had they not been subjected to the whims of the powerful, those four human beings might have even been happy.

When the head of the family suggested that he stay with them and share their work and the fruits of their labor, the exile rejected the offer, but he did so not because of their humble existence, but because he knew that his destiny was not to settle comfortably at some place along the way, but to continue his journey to the end.

When he took his leave, his bags were full. They hadn't been able to give him anything for his work except food, but for him it was more than enough payment.

Although initially the exile held strictly to the rule of traveling at night and avoiding being seen during the day, the truth is that little by little, as the days went by he became more careless. First, he got close enough to the roads so that he could see them from a distance. Then as he continued his journey, he moved almost imperceptibly to the ditch that ran on the side of the road. Finally, he walked on the road itself like any other unconcerned traveler.

He began to enjoy the sun and the air and the scenery and the flight of the birds. Even running to a tree to take shelter when it rained gave him a delicious sense of freedom. The journey had ceased to be a means to an end and become an experience in itself, one that, despite the privations, was actually pleasurable.

That was how after several days, the exile arrived at a small city. It was a haphazardly shaped settlement located on top of a hill and separated from where the exile was standing by a stone bridge. He thought that quite possibly the construction was from the time of the Romans and that this place had been inhabited for centuries and even millennia.

After many weeks of wandering through rugged country, seeing the city gave him a strange feeling. It was not as big as Valladolid, Seville, or Toledo, but even so it was a city, not a small village, and its buildings appeared well built and sound. For a moment, he wondered whether it would be wiser to go around and avoid it, but this time the exile's curiosity outweighed his good sense.

He descended the gentle slope that led to the bridge and crossed it with a determined step. Just for a moment he leaned over to look at the choppy stream, full of rocks, that flowed beneath the bridge. He remembered that just a few days ago, another bridge had saved his life and wondered if that was a good omen.

His gaze was so fixed on the road which zigzagged up towards the city that he did not notice the two guards who stood at the door of a casemate to the left of the bridge. But they saw him.

Looking down as if searching for something, they let him pass without a word or gesture. The exile was intent on saving his breath and reaching the city gate with enough strength. He was pleased to be able to reach the top of the hill, feel the air hitting him in the face, and note he was indeed stronger now than when he had been forced into exile. For a few moments, he felt not only happy but powerful. Yes, powerful. It was as if at that moment, the entire world with everything in it were at his command.

"Hey! You!" The shout that sounded behind him brought the exile out of his self-absorbed reverie.

"You! I'm talking to you!" the voice said again, and the exile turned to see whom he was talking to.

"Yes, you!" he heard, as a guard with a helmet on his head pointed at him with his right index finger.

The exile looked around to see if the guard might be addressing someone else, but didn't have a chance to find out. The guard took a few steps towards him and with a shove to the chest pushed him to the ground.

"Are you deaf, man?" the guard growled.

The exile tried to look up and see the man who had just assaulted him, but the sun was shining directly in his face. Instinctively, he put his hand to his eyes as a makeshift visor so that he could clearly view his assailant.

"What's the matter?" shouted the guard, kicking him in the leg. "Are you covering your face in case I punch you?"

"No, sir," replied the exile in the most respectful tone he could muster.

He tried to get up but felt the guard's boot on his chest, pushing him to the ground once more.

"Did I give you permission to get up?" he asked the exile.

With that the exile understood that the man had not made any mistake. This was how he behaved, and it was deliberate.

He noticed that the guard had a sword hanging from his swordbelt and carried a dagger on his right side. He knew that only the most measured prudence would save him from this situation. This situation? What situation was it in fact? Could they have recognized him as a fugitive of the Holy Office? But how? And in another kingdom?

"Tell me what you want, sir, and I will comply," replied the exile with a tone deferential enough to avoid being hit again.

The guard frowned. Perhaps he had expected resistance from the exile and was surprised by his compliant attitude. For the moment, he put his hand to his beard and stroked it thoughtfully. Yes, it seemed as though he had not expected this response.

"Stand up; I am taking you to the constable," he said at last.

The exile felt his heart sink. He tried to reassure himself that they couldn't possibly have recognized him, but he couldn't rid himself of the anxiety that arose in his heart. In any case, he had no choice but to obey. Once on his feet, he bowed his head and humbly said: "Tell me where I need to go."

Again a strange expression appeared on the guard's face. Definitely, the exile concluded, this man was not used to this kind of behavior. If anything, he was used to protests and even some resistance. But the exile would not allow himself to behave like that.

The guard motioned with his chin and the exile started off. As he walked, he turned to see if the armed individual was following him. Indeed, he was. And that is how they arrived at a building that looked very much like the place where city guards were garrisoned.

"Go on in," said the guard who was escorting him, in a weary tone.

The exile obeyed. An unpleasant chill engulfed him as soon as he crossed the narrow threshold. In a cubicle to the right, two guards played cards amidst shouts and bursts of laughter. They were certainly having fun, but they interrupted their entertainment when they saw the exile.

"Who is this, Jean?" one of them asked, addressing the man who had detained the exile.

"A smart aleck who crossed the bridge without paying," he replied contemptuously.

The two guards put their cards on the table as they exchanged looks of nasty amusement.

"They never learn, do they?" said one of them as he got up and took down a bunch of keys hanging on the wall.

The exile felt a shove to his back that almost made him fall headlong. And when the man with the keys stepped in front of him and began to move down the corridor, he concluded that it was a sign of where he should go.

With each step it got colder and damper, until he felt as if the chill were grabbing him by the throat and pounding his spine with a hammer. It was certainly a most unpleasant place. His impression worsened when the man who went ahead of him began to descend a stone staircase. Lord Almighty! If the cold was like this at ground level, what would it be like underground?

Before beginning the descent, the man had removed a torch from the wall and plunged into the oppressive darkness. The exile noted the dangerously slippery steps with concern, and he instinctively spread his hands towards the walls to keep from falling. The worst thing that could happen to him right now would be to end up with a sprained ankle or a broken leg.

They came to a corridor with a low ceiling, where the exile prudently lowered his head to avoid bumping it. He could barely see the circle of light surrounding the flickering flame of the torch. He knew that the guard was following behind him, but only by the sound of his footsteps.

"Here we are," said the man ahead of him. "We have arrived."

Then he fumbled through the bunch of keys in his hand until he found the one he was looking for and inserted it into the lock. The harsh screeching of the hinges was a prelude to the stench of sweat, urine, and filth that met them. The exile understood that this was the place where they were going to lock him up, but upon hearing some grunting from within, he realized that it could not be one of the dungeons of the Holy Office. It was evidently an ordinary prison, and despite the horrifying prospect, he was relieved. It was bad, very bad, but it could have been worse. And that is how life is, after all.

But he didn't have much time for reflection. Before he knew it, someone—most likely the guard behind him—yanked off his shoulder bags, and at the same time the man with the keys shoved him into the darkness. The door had not yet closed completely behind him when he heard the guard say:

"One way or the other, we will keep everything he has."

"Ha ha!" replied the other. "A nice prize indeed."

CHAPTER 6

Just as he had feared from the beginning, he had to wait to appear before the judge. How long? It was very difficult for him to answer that question exactly. Only a small window located at the end of a sloping wall made it possible to sense if it was still daylight or if the darkness of the night had already fallen. Unfortunately, sleepiness, dozing, and the fact that a fellow inmate had managed to clamber over to it in search of fresh air prevented him from having a clear idea of the passage of time.

When they finally called for him, the exile was filthy. He reeked all over, and his hair and beard had turned into a mass more like burlap than anything belonging to a human being.

When seen in the light, he found that his shoes and clothing were covered with a great assortment of stains. From what? He really couldn't say. Vomit, urine, excrement, dirt ... all mixed together. The judge was certainly going to have to be very discerning to see that he was not a tramp.

"Go upstairs," said the jailer after taking him out of the cell.

He realized that in all that time, no one had asked him his name, and then he understood the key to his arrest. They knew he was there, of course, and now they were taking him out of confinement, but they were not really interested in his name but only what they could get out of him. The question was whether a judge would right that wrong, and if not, how much they would be content with.

When he reached the upper floor, which was gloomy, dark, and damp, he nevertheless seemed to revive somewhat. No matter how you looked at it, it was much more bright, ventilated, and hospitable than what he had endured in the previous days. Life had those ironies. What is simply horrible and squalid may seem reasonably good to us when we come from someplace truly dreadful.

When the light from the doorway to the street hit him, it felt like a fingernail was scraping his pupils. In truth, he was so dazed that he hardly noticed when they shackled his hands and feet. One more shove and he was totally exposed to the sunlight. With that he felt excruciating pain in his eyes, a clamp-like pressure on his temples, and an overpowering urge to cover his already closed eyelids with his hands.

"Move it! Get going! We can't stand here all day!" he heard and tried to start walking. However, he had never been chained in his whole life, and he stumbled and almost fell to the ground.

"Let's go! Come on!" the guard prodded him.

The exile managed to look through tearing eyes and realized that the person leading him to God knows where was the same individual who had detained him a few days earlier. He was walking beside him and now he could better see his features. He was a little shorter than he, slim, with large hands. His pinched face, with thin but ugly features, ended in a pointy beard.

Then he saw that the man's nose was covered with a hideous wart. Of course, many people have warts and it is not of great importance, especially if they are not visible to the eye, but that henchman wasn't a man with a wart, but more like a wart with a man attached to it! He had not realized it days ago when the man had pushed him, treated him with a lack of consideration and in general behaved wretchedly towards him, but now in the sunlight ... before he realized it, he heard himself saying:

"Sir, if you ever want to get rid of what you have on your nose, I can help you with that."

The guard jerked his face around while his eyes reflected a mix of surprise and anger.

"I have knowledge of the healing arts," the exile hastened to say. "And for you, I would be willing to practice them for free, as ... as a token of gratitude and goodwill."

The guard's eyebrows shot up with an expression halfway between surprise and hope. He opened his mouth as if to say something and paused for an instant, but immediately closed it before a single sound came out. He remained silent, although a range of expressions played on his face until they came to a building made of white stone.

"Here we are," said the guard, but this time his tone of voice was very different. Then he added:

"Wait."

The exile blinked when he realized that the guard was now talking to him using a formal mode of address. Maybe ... just maybe...

"Let's go," he said, keeping the same form of respect. "Go on in."

They plowed through the doorway and stretching out before them was a dimly lit corridor crowded with other people—mostly men—who were weighed down with chains like him.

"We will wait until they call us," the henchman said, and immediately added:

"This can take a long time, so I advise you to sit on the floor or lean against the wall."

The exile chose the second option. Standing on his feet was something he appreciated after days spent in confinement. He needed to stretch his limbs more than he needed to rest.

Fortunately, they didn't have to wait long. There were maybe six or seven people ahead of him, but for the exile the fact that he could see things that were several lengths away, breathe purer air, and look around him was enough to make him happy, which eased his discomfort. Finally, he heard the guard tell him it was his turn.

The room they entered was small. A man he identified as the judge was sitting on a platform facing them. One step below, to the right and to the left, were two men who might be the prosecutor and the defense attorney, although the exile did not know who was who and what they could possibly say, since at no time had they exchanged a single word with him. Finally, next to a table overflowing with papers, was another individual whom the exile assumed was the court clerk.

The judge passed his hand over his face, like a self-satisfied caress.

"Who is next?" he asked.

"This man, Your Honor," said the henchman.

"What has he done?" asked the judge with troubling indifference.

"He crossed the bridge without paying the pontage," replied the guard.

"I see," said the judge. "He didn't pay the bridge toll. Did he protest? Put up a fight?"

"The truth is, no, Your Honor," replied the man with the wart, causing the judge to raise an eyebrow in surprise.

"No, huh?" the judge commented. "Well, he still committed a very serious crime. Very serious indeed. We have to protect the bridge. Not just anyone can cross it and besides ... well, nobody can enter to enjoy this magnificent city ... for free..ee."

He left the word floating in the air like a kite and then resumed his discourse.

"The accused will have to pay the toll, plus fifty percent as a fine for breaking the law, plus a one hundred percent surcharge. Does the defendant have assets to pay the amount?"

The exile tried to say something, but the guard preempted him.

"We seized a few shoulder bags with some shirts, a couple of books, and some instruments of what could be his profession. The books and the instruments..."

"You can keep the books," interrupted the judge. "Did he have a mount, a wagon, a pushcart... something else ...?"

"No, Your Honor," replied the guard, "Only what I have told you."

"That seems too little. Yes, too little. What can we do... we only have what God gives. I decree that everything he had on him be confiscated, including the boots he is wearing... they don't look too bad. Since there is still a difference that must be paid... yes, a difference, he will spend two months working on municipal projects. And since he will have to be fed and housed during that time... he will spend another month to pay for that. Does the accused have anything to say?"

"Your Honor," the exile began, "when I crossed the bridge, no one said anything about paying a pontage. I would have gladly paid it or I would not have entered the city. In addition, I consider that the surcharge and the fine..."

"You have nothing to consider," interrupted the judge.

"In that case, I would like to appeal to..."

"There is no other judge," the magistrate interrupted again.

"Then perhaps the mayor...," the exile stammered.

"I am the mayor," said the judge with a smirk.

"But..." the exile tried in vain to reason.

"I am the judge, I am the one who governs this city, and I am the one who makes the rules; and because I make them, they are fair. Indeed they are exceptionally fair."

The exile felt as if a thick black cloak settled over him. What kind of city was this where a single man made the laws, implemented them, and enforced them? All power was in the hands of one person! What possibility of justice could there be in a place like this?

The thud of the gavel against the table declaring that the sentence would be carried out jolted him back to reality. Before he knew it he was out on the street again, escorted by the guard.

"Don't worry," said the guard once they were outside. "Municipal work is much better than the place where you have been locked up. Of course, you will continue to sleep there, but while you work, you will get to breathe fresh air."

At any other time, the exile would have given his full attention to the guard's explanation and even felt relief. However, at that moment it was totally impossible. At the end of the street, he had just recognized three riders. Sweat soaked the palms of his hands and an unbearable weight settled on his chest. So these were the men who had been hunting him for weeks in order to take his life.

CHAPTER 7

Swiftly, the exile turned to face the guard and said, "It may not interest you, but I assure you that I can remove that wart."

"Well..."

The guard wasn't able to say anything more. The exile turned his back to the riders as he grabbed the guard's head in his hands and leaned over it just enough to hide most of his face.

"Let me take a look at it now in daylight," he said as he deftly shifted the angle of his body so that the riders could not see him.

For a few moments he carefully palpated the guard's nose, all the while listening intently to the sound of hooves from the horses of those who had been pursuing him for months. He uttered muffled grunts and deep sighs, as if he were examining something truly remarkable. Only when he did not hear anything anymore did the exile say:

"Two weeks."

"What?" the guard asked as he stroked his face, finally free from the exile's fingers.

"I only need two weeks to remove that wart," he stated as decisively as possible.

"Are ... are you sure?" the guard stammered.

"Yes, absolutely," the exile replied, nodding emphatically.

"And ... and just how much would it cost?" the guard inquired somewhat fearfully.

"Nothing," replied the exile with a smile. "Absolutely nothing. It will be on the house. No, don't say a word. I don't intend to change my mind."

"Well...," said the henchman with a satisfied grin on his gaunt face. "It sounds good ... I ... well, I ... I could find you a good job to do..."

For the first time since arriving in the city, the exile experienced a sense of relief. If his pursuers were only passing through, he would surely be safe by working for a few days for the municipality. In addition, the distance between them would increase again during that time. All things considered, it might turn out that the arrest had saved his life.

"You'll have to do what I tell you to," the guard said as they walked.

"Of course," replied the exile.

The following days were, without a doubt, the best of his captivity. His captor spoke to the men who were watching over him and made sure they gave him a quiet job. He convinced them that it was not worthwhile to make the exile carry sand and stones when he knew how to read, write, and reckon accounts, and was therefore able to take over all of their own duties.

By the end of three days, the men had come to the firm conclusion that the new inmate was the best thing that had happened to them in a long time. They improved his food rations and, by the second week, even allowed him to sleep outside the dungeon with the rationale that he could continue to keep accounts and perform other duties at night.

They were not the only ones satisfied with the exile's presence. In fact, as far as his captor was concerned ... either he was sorely mistaken, or his wart would fall off in a couple of weeks.

During those weeks, the exile understood as never before the extraordinary value of things that are routinely overlooked. He discovered the pleasure of breathing fresh air, the contentment of working without confinement, the delight of eating food that tasted better than what he had been consuming shortly before, the satisfaction of seeing others appreciate his work, the joy of being unshackled.

To tell the truth, on more than one occasion he thought that being confined to that work, he was freer than in other times of his life. Yes, he was serving a sentence, but in a few weeks he would embrace complete freedom, as he would have embraced his mother or, if he had had one, his wife.

Even more importantly, during those weeks not the slightest hint of bitterness or resentment welled up in his heart. Perhaps it was simply because he was too happy serving his sentence to experience the slightest ill will towards anyone. Why worry about others when he knew he would soon resume his journey to freedom? And so the days went by.

One morning, the guard who had arrested him a few weeks before said, "It's time for you to leave."

"Are you sure?" the exile replied while examining with satisfaction the empty spot the wart had left on the guard's nose.

"Yes, yes..." the guard answered nervously. "Come with me."

A smile of joy appeared on the exile's face as he contemplated the man's nervousness. It would be nice if in the end he would actually miss him...

They walked together towards the road out of town, neither of them saying anything. They reached the gate on the other side of the city from the one through which he had entered a few weeks earlier. For the first time, the exile could see that the descent was more gradual than on the other side and that it continued all the way until it joined a path that ran parallel to a forest. It was the ideal place to get lost, the exile told himself, and resume his journey.

He had barely passed through the gate when the guard said to him, "You obviously do not know the rules of this city, sir."

The exile was surprised by the guard's form of address. At no time had he called him "sir." He thought that maybe the wart must have been more unbearable to him than he had imagined.

"In this city, no one is ever released," the guard continued, looking down in shame. "Once everything a person has is taken away, he is never free again. When he is released, we proceed to arrest him again, accuse him of something, anything, take away what little he has left, and make him a slave for as long as we please..."

The henchman looked up and fixed his gaze on the exile. A shadow of regret hung over his eyes, watery now, a regret that must have been overwhelming and painful.

"Sir," the guard continued, "right now I should detain you again... and ... and there would be no appeal because..."

"Because the mayor, the judge, and the lawmaker are one and the same."

The guard agreed silently with a slight nod of his head.

"What awaits me?" asked the exile, his heart pounding painfully against his chest.

"Freedom, sir, only freedom," replied the guard as he slipped his right hand inside his cloak.

The exile was stunned to see that the man offered him the same shoulder bags he had taken away from him a few weeks earlier.

"The only things inside are your books and ... and your boots," he said.

The exile realized that this man, who until then had been a cog in a corrupt machine, was handing over the spoils he had received the day the exile had been sentenced.

"I would have liked to recover more items, but..."

"It is more than enough," the exile interrupted him, "more than enough."

"I have also included a loaf of bread," added the guard.

"Thank you," said the exile, "thank you very very much. I would like to..."

"You need to hurry, sir," the guard interrupted him.

The exile nodded and started to turn around. Then unexpectedly, he said:

"Your nose looks much better now."

The guard smiled, touched the place left by the wart, and said:

"Do you really think so?"

CHAPTER 8

It was upon being released from prison and leaving the city that the exile began to reflect on everything he had not really thought about during his incarceration. Time and again, his questions ended up leading to a fundamental one: how had he come to be denounced in the first place? After much thought, he concluded that things had begun to spiral downward the day he decided to help Fernando.

That round-faced, ruddy young man had never been more than a poor wretch. His father had died in one of the ruthless raids the Moors frequently carried out against the eastern coast. He was still a small child at the time, but after the tragedy the authorities of the kingdom had not helped either his widowed mother or him. Finally, the poor woman decided to leave the east of the country and head inland to the plateau. After numerous twists and turns, they ended up in a town close to that of the exile.

There, Fernando grew in height and girth, but not in good sense. For years he was coddled by a possessive mother, who was determined to prevent him from growing up so that he would never disappear from home as her husband had done. His mother was tormented by the pain of marital loss and clung to superstitions. The fruit of that suffocating upbringing was a lily livered, capricious, and choleric young man.

One day, the immature young man got a girl pregnant in the town's threshing grounds. The result was a hasty and unhappy marriage. Suddenly, Fernando found himself lowering his heavy bull-like forehead before the continuous reprimands of a mother who refused to stop exercising her dominance. At the same time his wife increasingly made more bitter complaints against the open despotism of her mother-in-law.

Frequent, bitter quarrels ensued, which soon, very soon, culminated in brutal slaps and blows that an enraged Fernando inflicted on his wife. She in turn did not cease to shriek out her bitter disappointment.

A son, whom they named José, was born to the couple, and he quickly became the basket into which the parents threw all of their bitterness. Fernando dealt him blow after blow, as if in so doing he could escape the fate that tormented him.

As for José's mother, she regarded him with increasing hatred because she had come to the conclusion that without him her life would surely have been happy and, above all, distant from the brutal husband with whom she shared a bed and her fate.

It is hardly possible to think of a more unfortunate, more miserable, and more desperate quartet than the one formed by the mother-in-law, the couple, and the young son. Hence it is not surprising that the wife turned to wine to try to drown her deep, unspeakable pain.

The life of the exile had intersected with that of Fernando quite by chance. For some time, he had taken pleasure in retiring to a pine forest near town and devoting himself to reading quietly, far away from meddlesome eyes. He had always been cautious when indulging in this delectable pastime, but that afternoon he was so absorbed in his reading that he did not notice Fernando nearby. When he finally noticed the intrusive shadow that fell next to him, the round-faced young man with a ruddy beard had been peering at him for a good while.

"God be with you," he said, more to show that he had noticed him than because he wished him well.

"God be with you, too," Fernando replied, and then immediately asked: "What are you reading, sir?"

He was tempted to avoid giving him an answer and send him away in the most courteous and firm way possible. Nevertheless, his desire to share the joy sparked by what he had been reading that afternoon overruled his prudence.

Thus, little by little, as if he had known Fernando all his life, he began to share with him the noble and pure ideas that emerged from the book. He spoke to him of a God who was not found in temples made by human hands, but who wanted to come into every human heart. He described to him how, as much as they wanted to deny it, the children of men were wayward and lost creatures who needed refuge amidst the sad unfolding of their existence. He expressed how it was essential to look with compassion on all those who cross our paths in this world.

He did not recognize at any point that with each word and phrase he exposed a part of himself that could be used against him and make him liable to being burned to death. He had been talking for a good while when Fernando blurted out:

"Perhaps you can help me, sir..."

At a time like this, someone else might have smelled danger, but that was not the case with the exile. On the contrary, he listened carefully to the string of misfortunes that Fernando recounted in rapid succession. The unwanted pregnancy, the forced marriage, the acrimony of a drunken wife, the rebellious and hated son, the new offspring his wife was carrying, the sick and unstable mother, everything gushed out of the mouth of Fernando, this young man with shifty eyes and a dull face.

The exile listened to it all with attention and sorrow, with the kind of sadness that arises when contemplating the misery of others. Before he knew it, he was offering Fernando an occasional job to help him put food on the table. He was motivated by a commendable feeling of charity and, of course, he did not suspect that his generosity was the beginning of an unequal and asymmetric relationship that would have profound consequences.

For the next two years, time and again, the man who could not even imagine that he would end up as an exile sought ways to help this sullen, bitter, and, as he soon discovered, not very hard-working man.

The exile would invent tasks for Fernando or pay him to carry out tasks that he himself could have done without cost in his free time. He never needed Fernando to work for him, but he acted out of deep pity for the unfortunate young man, for the woman in the clutches of wine, for José who continued to be slapped and shoved around, and for the two new little ones, a boy and a girl, who were born in successive years.

In the conversations they sometimes shared, Fernando tried to understand what the future exile was explaining to him, but it was not difficult for his conversational partner to understand that this man with the round face and ruddy beard was not one of those who sought God to understand themselves and the world in which they lived. Rather, he belonged to the group of people who seek to use the Creator as a hammer to strike the head of anyone they want to destroy.

The exile was also astonished to discover that Fernando often did not carry out the tasks entrusted to him but instead gave them to his wife to do.

That discovery happened at about the same time Fernando told him he was visiting the parish priest more than ever before. What happened next was an accelerated process that he should not have ignored. Fernando continued to come to his house in search of some remuneration, but his supposed interest in the views of the future exile had given way to a different attitude.

It seemed as if blinders hid behind his narrow forehead that only allowed him to see black and white. Suddenly, he began to view everything bad that happened to him—from his inability to move forward in life to the illness that had befallen his mother and the increasing waywardness of his son—as direct results of the spiritual guilt of others.

In the kingdom, according to the young man, there lurked people who had fallen away from what the priests taught, thereby placing everyone under the threat of God's wrath. In other words, life treated Fernando badly not because he had been unable to control himself and thereby avoid getting his girl-friend pregnant, or because he remained unashamedly lazy, or because he had not learned to behave like a man, or because he continued to hang on to his mother's skirts, but rather because the Almighty was punishing the land, and that included him, due to hidden heretics.

Hearing those arguments expressed in a voice suffused with poorly concealed anger, the future exile could not help but feel fear, but at the same time, it was impossible for him to stop feeling deep compassion for the suffering that gripped Fernando's monstrously twisted soul.

Some time later, he would wonder if that situation, which was deteriorating day by day, had not taken a huge downturn when Fernando decided to take his mother to the shrine of a supposedly miraculous virgin. The woman could barely move anymore, but her son loaded her into a cart and headed to the shrine. He had announced his plans the day before, and they both knew, even without saying a word about it, that the future exile viewed that show of superstition as useless and deplorable, while Fernando did not fully believe in what he was doing either. The woman died in excruciating pain just a few weeks after their return.

As soon as the poor woman was buried, Fernando communicated to the exile his aspirations to become an Informant of the Holy Inquisition. This time, the future exile kept silent. Did Fernando tell him that to provoke him, did he sincerely want to know his opinion, or was he looking for his approval? In reality it didn't matter. The fact was, Fernando wished to become part of that peculiar institution that extended its control throughout the kingdom. And the king himself did not dare oppose it.

The exile thought that maybe his decision was not so difficult to understand. Looking at the situation impartially, it was obvious that Fernando had neither natural talent nor education. Nor was he industrious or clever. All things said and done, he was no more than a spoiled sluggard who wanted fame and a position he could never achieve on his own merits or efforts.

As he reflected on the unvarnished reality of Fernando's character, a tight swirl of images quickly crowded into his mind of things he had overlooked until then. He remembered with clarity the way Fernando's half-closed eyes roamed over his modest house, his modest orchard, and his even more modest collection of books, and he understood then that that gaze had never been pure, curious, or genuinely interested, but simply envious.

That night, the future exile reached the painful and dreadful conclusion that on a day least expected, he would be denounced, and that it would happen by people who only wanted to take away what he had, concealing their greed under cover of the most fanatical religiosity.

CHAPTER 9

Piercing, heartrending, and almost animal-like cries reached the exile's ears as he was about to leave the forest and join the main road. Keeping his body hidden behind a tree, he observed a group of people where the weeping was coming from.

A priest holding a huge crucifix walked at the head. Behind him, two altar boys formed an escort, and together they were the vanguard for about a dozen people who were not wearing any liturgical garments. These were the ones who were both crying and making a huge effort to hold back their tears.

To all appearances they were coming from a burial. Turning his gaze to the right, he made out a whitewashed wall about a hundred paces away with crosses sticking up above it, which confirmed his first impression. Yes, they must be returning from an interment. This would explain the presence of the priest, his acolytes, and those poor people devastated by seemingly unbearable grief.

For a moment, the exile thought about joining the group. He probably would have done so at another time and in another place, but now.... He waited for the procession to continue ahead a little more and then he went out onto the road. Accustomed to traveling through the middle of the forest where the sun barely filtered down, the brightness of the sun hit him immediately. He did not think that the good weather would last long, but for as many days as it did, he would take advantage of it.

He had been walking for a while and keeping some distance from the funeral cortege when he caught a glimpse of a low, flat building that he thought might be an inn. Yes, it had all the appearance of being the type of establishment found near towns that offers services that are not always virtuous.

He was reflecting on this when he saw the priest stop at the door, hand the crucifix to the altar boys, and enter the building. All the members of the procession followed except the children who remained outside and very quickly started to play.

The exile should have continued on his way towards the town where he could decide to either circumvent it or risk entering. However, curiosity, a curiosity not chastened by any recent experience and developed during days of calm and safe travel, led him to stop.

"Are you coming from a funeral?" he asked the two altar boys.

The boys, who had leaned the crucifix against the wall, looked at each other, surprised that someone was speaking to them. Finally, the taller one replied:

"Uncle Jean's. He kicked the bucket."

"You shouldn't say he kicked the bucket," his companion rebuked him. "He means, sir, that he passed away."

The exile suppressed a smile at the boy's explanation.

"And what did he die of?" the exile inquired.

"The plague," replied the altar boy who had corrected his companion.

The exile felt a burst of anxiety rush through his breast when he heard that accursed word. The plague.... If those parts were infected by an epidemic, he needed to get out of there as soon as possible. Immediately, in fact.

He had reached that decision from a conversation that could be heard through the door of the inn that had been left ajar. Anyone could have closed it behind them, but for whatever reason they had left it open, and it was enough for the exile to hear what was being discussed inside the establishment.

"We don't have a choice, gentlemen," said an imperious and impatient voice. "No choice. Has the plague come to our city? Yes, it has. There is no doubt about that. We just came from the Christian burial of one of its victims."

A loud wail erupted at these words. Undoubtedly, it came from the widow or one of the children of the deceased.

"Well then," the voice continued, "we need do the best thing.... We must act now."

"What do you suggest, Father Louis?" he heard someone ask.

"The only thing that can be suggested," answered the imperious voice, "what anyone should suggest. What all villagers should be asking for: to carry the relic of the Holy Child Jesus in procession. His Holy Prepuce will save us from all these evils. I intend to speak to the mayor, and this Sunday, without further delay, I will gather all the people after High Mass to follow the holy relic through the town. Then I will offer it to everyone so they can kiss it."

The exile felt a shiver of horror when he heard that. He knew without a doubt that what the priest intended to do would lead to a massive spread of the disease and an incalculable number of deaths.

He wanted to believe that the person in question did not understand it, but the truth was that he was opening the door for the plague to wipe out all or most of the population. The exile knew that definitely the most prudent thing to do was to get away from there before it became a center of uncontainable death. He promptly waved goodbye to the two altar boys and hurried away.

It was not long before he reached a fork in the road. Straight ahead lay the town that was most likely the one at risk of disappearing; on the right, he could see the road gently curve, heading to another place that was hidden from view.

The exile felt inclined to take that bypass and, in fact, began to direct his steps towards it. However, he didn't get far. Something inside told him that he could not leave without trying to help those people who were much closer to death than they could ever have imagined.

He stopped and stood as if his feet were nailed to the road. But it was only an instant because at once he sighed deeply and turned to go in the direction of the plague-ridden city.

He was already near when he saw the funeral procession in the distance, with the priest and the altar boys at the front.

They must have refreshed themselves and were already returning home. That accorded a special urgency to his steps.

He entered the city and immediately stopped the first person he met to ask for the town hall. It was not far away and, in fact, he had to ask only one more person to find it.

The town hall was an oblong, two-story building with whitewashed walls and exposed wooden beams. It was a simple construction, but not entirely ugly. A guard stood at the door, topped with a helmet and armed with a spear. There was no doubt this was the place.

"Sir," said the exile, "I must speak to the mayor."

The guard looked at him in amazement. Nothing in the exile's attire gave him reason to give him access to the mayor.

"I am a physician," added the exile, "and I believe my services are needed in this city."

The sentry looked at him with distrust, but this time he paid attention.

"Wait here a moment," he said, indicating with his palm that he should not move from where he was standing.

The exile obeyed and watched the guard go into the interior of the building. He didn't have to wait long. Indeed, in scant time the guard returned to the door and motioned for the exile to enter.

"I don't understand why, to be honest, but the mayor wants to see you."

They climbed a wooden staircase and went down a narrow corridor flanked by windows. They walked along until the guard signaled for him to stop. Then he used his knuckles to knock on a door in front of him. A shout from the inside indicated that they could go in.

The exile walked into a wide, spacious room that opened onto a balcony. In the center was a large table with two chairs resting in front, and a frail man with a grizzled beard and incipient baldness sitting behind it. To the right was a desk where possibly a clerk would sit. On the left he detected a cabinet, likely used for keeping documents.

"Who are you and what is it you want?" asked the man sitting behind the table, with a hint of impatience.

"I am a doctor, sir," replied the exile. "As I was heading north, I ran into a funeral procession that came from burying someone from this town. I then learned that the plague threatens this place, and I decided I could serve you by helping to prevent the disease from spreading."

The exile spoke in a courteous and firm manner, yet entirely devoid of arrogance or the usual smoothness of charlatans.

The man sitting behind the table stroked his beard thoughtfully. It looked like he was surprised by the arrival of the exile and even more by his unexpected offer. He was silent for a few moments and then finally said:

"To the best of your knowledge and belief, what do you think we should do?"

"It is very simple, sir," replied the exile. "First, you must identify those already infected. That first step is essential because the second is to isolate them so that they cannot spread the disease to others. Next, people have to stay in their homes until the plague passes. During that time, they have to follow some essential rules of cleanliness. If they do so, I can assure you that the disease will pass. The number of deaths will no longer go up, and then they will cease."

"And you are sure of that because you are a doctor, of course..."

"That's right, sir," replied the exile. "I myself can examine the population to separate the infected from the healthy and thus ensure that the plague does not spread."

"And what would you need?" the mayor inquired with a hint of mistrust in his voice.

"I would need a tailor to make me a garment according to the instructions I give him, which will protect me from contagion."

"What do you want to receive in return for your work?" the mayor then asked.

The exile suddenly realized that he had not thought this far. He should have, without a doubt, but the truth was that this vital point had not even crossed his mind.

"I will accept whatever you yourself consider fair," he ended up answering.

The mayor smiled in satisfaction when heard his answer. Whatever happened, it was up to him to decide how to pay this unexpected individual.

"But on two conditions," added the exile, removing the smirk from the mayor's face.

"Which are..."

"The first is that I will be able to leave this job whenever I see fit."

"And when do you think that will be, may I ask?"

"When everyone has been cured or when it becomes impossible to carry out my work in the appropriate way."

"So be it," the mayor accepted. "And the second?"

"That I am allowed to work in peace, as I choose, without interference from anyone."

The mayor was silent and stroked his beard again as he rose from his chair.

"I'll be frank with you," he said. "The doctor we had died. And to tell you the truth, quite possibly the group you saw returning from the cemetery was the one who buried him. We are in great need and I will not hide it. You have made a good impression on me ... and I accept your conditions."

The exile bowed his head in respect and then said: "When can I start?"

"When would you like to?"

"As soon as I have the proper clothing to protect myself from the plague and can begin examining the residents."

"Well then, today. This man will accompany you to the tailor's house, and you can give him the necessary instructions."

The exile left the town hall still in disbelief of what had just transpired.

CHAPTER 10

There was some wariness—no doubt inevitable—when the locals saw the newly arrived doctor dressed in the peculiar clothing the tailor had fashioned for him. Covered with a mask made of thick fabric that extended into an artificial nose with glasses mounted on it, and a dark robe that reached down to his feet, the exile went visiting house by house in search of the sick.

With astonishing aplomb, the exile ordered the sick to be separated, dwellings closed, and even belongings burned. But fear was so thick it choked throats and squeezed hearts with its iron hand, and hardly anyone dared to express more than amazement and surprise.

In less than a week, the hard-working exile, who seemed capable of not sleeping at all, had managed to stop the spread of the disease, in the same way that Jehovah's command had stopped the sword of the angel of death when it was mowing down the Egyptians. The rigorous identification of the sick, the total isolation of the infected, the strict, obligatory hygienic measures all had an immediate effect on the town. For a few days, people had continued to die, but little by little, the number of deaths had decreased, and above all, new infections had stopped. A few dozen peasants were still ill, but the exile thought that he could save if not all, at least some of their lives.

One morning as the exile made his usual round of visits to the sick, he saw the outline of the mayor silhouetted in the doorway of the house where he was carrying out his healing work. He had not noticed his proximity, nor that he had been observing him for a while, and so he was a bit startled when he spotted him.

"What can I do for you?" the exile asked respectfully.

"May I speak with you?" asked the mayor.

"Yes, of course. Only let me finish examining this sick individual."

For the next few minutes, the exile felt the patient's bulging throat, took his temperature, examined his stool, listened to his breathing, and finally let out a hint of a smile that was more humble than satisfied.

"Don't forget to take the concoction that I prescribed for you," he reminded the patient.

"Yes, my daughter will bring it to me," said the sick man.

"But don't let her touch you or come near you," the exile insisted with mock severity.

"She never does."

The exile took leave of the sick man and approached the mayor, who was waiting for him outside the doorway.

"Tell me," the exile encouraged him when the two met in the street.

"We have not had much opportunity to speak during these days," the mayor began, "but I have to tell you that the municipality is very grateful to you."

The exile motioned with his hand to interrupt him, but the mayor continued:

"No, permit me to continue. What you have done for this community cannot be described in words. You are not seeking to profit from this, you have not asked for even a coin in advance, and you have asked for nothing more than a strange outfit that helps you to carry out your work. It would have been difficult, yes very difficult, to find someone as dedicated, hardworking, and selfless as you."

When he heard that litany of praise, an alarm went off inside the exile's head. It was not that he doubted the sincerity of the mayor's words, but suddenly he began to fear that after that verbal sweetness a blow was coming, a blow so crushing that he could not even begin to imagine it.

"Anyway ... I have no words to adequately express our gratitude," the mayor continued. "Precisely because of that ... precisely because of that, it is difficult for me..."

"What is it, Mr. Mayor?" the exile tried to help him.

The mayor stopped, took a deep breath, and then turned to the doctor.

"The parish priest insists on getting involved..."

The exile thought that the parish priest had never stopped being involved. He celebrated mass daily, he insisted on hearing confession up close to people, and he ignored the quarantine whenever he felt like it, all to display his rather considerable arrogance and total lack of common sense.

"Doctor, I need you to talk to him ... to listen to him.... Please come have lunch with him and me."

The exile was about to tell him that this was a breach of what was agreed upon before he began to render his services, but he remained silent. What was important, indeed essential above all, was the fate of these poor people.

He nodded and resumed walking when the mayor did so. Without saying another word, they reached the only inn that remained open in the town. It was half empty.

In silence, the mayor walked to a corner table and slumped onto a wooden bench. The exile took a seat across from him, and they continued in silence until the arrival of the priest a few moments later. The cleric entered the room with an air of command, superiority, confidence. His confidence seemed to puff him up so much that he almost floated.

"Blessed Mary, Mother of God," he said as he came to the table, but the invocation was only met with silence from the exile and a soft murmur from the mayor.

Exuding satisfaction, the priest sat down. Then he looked up and gestured for the innkeeper to come closer:

"What do you recommend for us today?" he said with a wide smile to the owner of the place.

"The trout," he said bowing to the priest, "is delicious today, Father, truly delicious."

"Bring me the trout then," said the cleric, pleased, "and a white wine from this area to wash them down with. And the best cheese you have."

"Of course, Father, of course," replied the innkeeper. "And the mayor?"

"I think I will also follow your recommendation," he replied.

"And what about the doctor?"

The exile did not say anything; he just nodded, showing that he agreed to the same order as the others.

The innkeeper had barely walked away when the priest rubbed his hands together lightly, as if wanting to warm up, and then plastered on a smile.

"I don't know, esteemed doctor," the priest began, "if the mayor has said anything to you..."

He paused for a moment, waiting for an answer, but the exile remained silent.

"Well, then ... regarding the plague that has devasted this town ... No one, least of all I, would not thank you for your toil, your immense toil in confronting it. I say it with all my heart, but ... but, well, I don't want to upset you, but it is evident that despite your efforts you have not been able to stop the spread of this evil. No, no, I don't blame you. It is only natural. These types of scourges originate in a supernatural world and must be overcome by supernatural means."

"What do you propose?" asked the exile, trying hard to contain the apprehension that had begun to grip him.

"To carry the Holy Prepuce of the Baby Jesus in procession," the priest said in a sharp voice, all his deference evaporating.

"Which one of them, Father?" the exile asked dryly.

"Which one? What do you mean, which one? The Holy Prepuce of the Baby Jesus!" answered the clergyman, spitting out each syllable.

"With all due respect," said the exile, "there is a prepuce of the Baby Jesus in Burgos. Yes, and another one in Rome. And also in Our Lady of Antwerp."

The priest opened his mouth as his eyebrows rose in enormous surprise.

"It is a problem, Father, I know," continued the exile, "but it is not the only problem. There is a head of Saint John the Baptist in Rome and another in Amiens, in France. Eusebius wrote that there were three nails of the cross. One was thrown into the Adriatic Sea by St. Helena, mother of the emperor Constantine, to calm the storm; the second she had melted into a helmet for her son, and the third she had made into a bit for his horse. As far as I know, and if my memory hasn't failed me, there are nails of the cross in Rome, Milan, Cologne, Paris, Lyons, and countless other places. There are over five hundred baby teeth of Our Lord on display in France alone. As for Our Lady's milk, Mary Magdalene's hair, Saint Christopher's molars, there's no counting them. I even know of a very ancient monastery where among the relics a part of the Brook Kidron is exhibited, although I cannot tell you with certainty whether it is water or pebbles from the creek. I could recite other more absurd and impious things, but I will only say that in a collegiate church, I was shown a rib from the Holy Savior. Whether or not there was another Savior besides Jesus Christ, and whether he left behind a rib or not, is something I leave to your consideration."

The parish priest opened and closed his mouth a few times, but was unable to get a word out. The exile, however, was unwilling to stop his discourse.

"I am not trying to tell you, Father, what to do in your church. Such a thought would never cross my mind. But as a physician, I am very concerned about the health of the people of this town, and that's why I'm going to tell you what will happen if you bring out that relic—the first, second, or third prepuce of the Baby Jesus that is found in Christendom. Of course people will stop quarantining and go out into the streets to kiss the relic that you will be holding in your hands. They will crowd together to get closer to the prepuce; they will leave their sweat and their spittle on the relic, and all that detritus will pass from one pair of lips to another, from one hand to another, from one body to another, causing the plague, which is already almost contained, to spread again, probably much more forcefully and with a much higher mortality than before. You believe that exhibiting the relic will promote the spiritual and physical health of your neighbors. I am not going to go into the question of spiritual health, but I have no doubt, not the slightest, that the effect on bodily health will be disastrous and that in a matter of days the dead will fill the streets. I am going to say it only once, that as a physician I consider carrying the relic of that prepuce in procession through the streets would most certainly cause terrible, mortal harm, and would allow the contagion to spread widely."

He had barely finished speaking when the dishes of trout were brought to the table. The priest put his hands together and began to utter a prayer in Latin. When he and the mayor crossed themselves, the exile did not move. Finally, the cleric said with a forced smile:

"I think we have both said what we had to say. Without a doubt, the Lord Mayor, who is a good Christian, will know which is the right decision."

Yes, the exile thought, *the mayor would surely know what the clergyman considered the right decision.* Whether that was the decision he should take for the good of the residents was another matter altogether.

The next two days were a bitter trial for the exile. The town crier regularly announced, following a meticulous schedule, that the relic of the Holy Prepuce of the Baby Jesus would be brought out and carried in procession to appease the wrath of God, so that the Almighty, who was already aggrieved, would put a stop to the disease.

The first time the exile heard the announcement, he felt a visceral disgust and then immediately after, an anger he had a hard time controlling. Perhaps it was true that the Lord was using that terrible scourge to carry out a rightful judgment. Perhaps. Who could ever know? But if that were the case, it was rather doubtful He would be moved by the exhibition of one of the many foreskins of the Baby Jesus that were scattered throughout the world.

No, God who created the mind, reason, and intellect wants them to be used, and among other purposes to be employed in holding back the advance of evil among men. It was indeed God and only God who endowed human beings with understanding so that they could build roofs to protect themselves from inclement weather, erect dams to avoid floods, design roads to travel on to other regions and bring people together in spite of distances, and apply elementary principles of health and hygiene to prevent a contagious disease from killing all of humanity. This reality, experienced time after time throughout the ages, could not be replaced by a superstition characteristic of the most abject paganism.

Overwhelmed by these reflections, the exile concluded that he must leave. He communicated this to the mayor one afternoon after a day of exhausting work that felt more futile than ever. He was convinced that all the grueling work he had done in the past few weeks would dissipate like the night dew at sunrise. The hours of steadfast effort, unending lack of sleep, and tireless work would be, like a dry twig thrown into the fire, reduced to ashes. Soon, all that would be left of a work carried out against all odds would be death.

The mayor understood his reasons. He did not say it, but it was obvious from the manner in which he looked down, as if he were ashamed of having committed a horrible sin.

When he observed that reaction the exile wondered if he still had a chance. He stopped talking, swallowed and decided to make one last attempt.

"Mr. Mayor, something critical is at stake here. We are not arguing about the authenticity of this or that relic. No. There is much more at stake than that. What we are discussing, Mr. Mayor, is whether these people, the people whom you have a duty to care for and protect, will all die or be saved, whether they will perish or come out alive from this plague. If people gather in that procession and crowd in to touch the relic and kiss it, then Mr. Mayor... this town could disappear."

He stopped speaking and looked at the mayor. The wrinkles on his forehead looked like deep slashes drawn with a sharp knife. It was obvious that a fierce battle was being waged in his heart, and the life of his neighbors was directly dependent on the outcome. He was silent for a few moments and finally opened his mouth:

"Doctor, I love this place more than you can imagine. My grandparents came here when I was not yet born. My parents, with great effort and much work, managed to make their way and then ... and then my two older sisters—who are now married and live elsewhere—and I came along. I love this place. I know its vineyards and its orchards. I have wept with the people when the harvest was poor, and I have caroused with them when it was abundant. I have felt the death of each neighbor as my own, and I have rejoiced with each new birth. Every one of these deaths I have felt here, deep in my breast."

The exile let him finish and then asked him the question on which everything hinged:

"What are you going to do, sir?"

The mayor closed his eyes, and the exile could clearly see two tears, huge and bright, slide down his cheekbones until they were lost in his beard.

"You ... you ..." he began in a muffled voice, "you cannot understand what the parish priest means in this town. Virtually everything that people know or understand about the world beyond these fields, they know or hear about from the pulpit. Yes, people think that ... they think they learn something on their own, but they only really know what that man tells them. He tells them how they should behave in their work, in their family ... even in bed! He tells them what they can eat or drink, with whom they can or cannot sleep, what they are allowed to wear, what they need to reject ... even what to burn. When the harvest is good, he attributes it to his prayers for which he charges a good amount; when it is bad, he demands that more prayers be offered, which also have a cost. When a child dies at birth, he says it is a punishment from God; when it comes into this world healthy and strong, he also attributes it to God and, in both cases, demands suitable payment for His Representative, which is himself. Even death cannot break that chain because as soon as an unfortunate individual has breathed his last, the priest offers the family the assurance that he will spend less time suffering in purgatory thanks to the Holy Masses that will be celebrated in his name—for a payment of course."

The mayor stopped and passed his right hand over his mouth as if to clean his lips of what had just come from them. For a moment he was silent. Then he let out a deep sigh and resumed his reflection.

"To be honest, I don't think the blame for all this comes from the priest. He is not a bad man, believe me. No, he is not. It is true that he is a little ... arrogant, but he is not the culprit. At least, not the direct culprit. All this comes from way back and from people who for centuries have bowed their heads in submission. Not even the kings have managed to change this state of affairs ... Do you really believe, sir, that I, a simple mayor, a humble mayor, a ... lowly ... mayor ... could accomplish that? Do you really believe so?"

The exile felt immense sorrow as the mayor laid out his perspective. He certainly was not a bad man either. Yes, he was surely sincere in his love for the people of his town. Certainly that was all true, but even if he were the purest of saints, the truth was that he was making a decision that would annihilate them all.

"Mr. Mayor," the exile said in the calmest tone possible, "if these people throng together in the procession, if they touch and kiss that prepuce ... the only thing that will come of it is massive contagion. Everything we have done so far will come crashing down. Everything. Neither the priest nor anyone, not even you, will have the least chance of surviving the plague. If that weren't the case, I..."

"You are going to leave," the mayor interrupted him. "I remember the terms of our agreement."

The mayor put his hand to his waist and took out a bag that he held out to the exile.

"I know all too well that this does not even begin to pay for the work you have done, but I beg you to accept it as a token of recognition for all that you have done for this community."

"But ...," the exile tried to reason, still believing that there was a small possibility of averting disaster.

"Sir," the mayor cut him off, "please accept it. Nothing else can be done."

The exile watched as the mayor bowed his head in respect and gave him one last look.

"God be with you," the mayor said softly before turning and walking away.

The exile would have liked to say goodbye as well, but before he could open his mouth, the mayor had quickened his pace and disappeared in the distance.

The night was heavy with sorrow for the exile. He should have slept in preparation for resuming his interrupted journey, but sleep fled from him like a hare that discovers a hunter close by. In the few moments he was able to doze, he was troubled by dreams of Fernando, Alfonso, his brother, others who had caused him trouble during his journey, the priest, and the many people he had treated throughout recent days. It was not a well-ordered dream, but rather, a string of seemingly disconnected and almost always disturbing images.

When the rooster crowed its song into the air to proclaim the dawn, the exile had already been up for a long time.

He waited for the sun to rise before eating. He broke his fast calmly, quietly, deliberately, as if he wanted to enjoy every piece of bread and every sip of milk.

Then he returned to his room, divided the money he had received between the shoulder bags, his pockets, and his boots and decided to set off. He went out into the street, took a deep breath, and realized that this was the last time he would see that town. He did not intend to return, but even if he did, it was doubtful he would find anything alive in its streets or fields.

With the burden of that premonitory sorrow pressing on his heart, he began to walk on the road leading out of town and thus arrived at the square where the church stood. During the previous days when he had taken charge of the health of the residents, the place had remained empty. Now the area in front of the church was full of people. Not overflowing nor packed enough to fill the porticos of nearby buildings or to block the way, but still full.

The exile paused for a moment and looked at them. Suddenly, the priest emerged from the church followed by two acolytes as the murmur of the people rose to an eloquent shout. Now the clergyman was not carrying a crucifix like the first time he had seen him. Instead, he held a small chest in his hands. To the exile, his expression seemed to be more full of pleasure than of devotion.

"Neighbors!" he heard him shout. "We are gathered here to celebrate this act of redress towards God whom we have seriously offended. *Paternoster...*"

The exile heard him recite the Our Father in Latin followed by a Hail Mary and a Gloria also in the language of Cicero. Then he extended his arms, holding out the chest and shouted:

"Here is the Holy Prepuce of the Baby Jesus, a most holy relic that has come down to us from time immemorial. Let us give it our devotion so that the Lord God Most High and Merciful will receive this act of redress."

As if by a spring, the inhabitants launched themselves forward to kiss the relic. Indeed, they would have knocked the priest down if it had not been for a pair of guards armed with spears who forced them to line up.

For a moment, the exile watched as the people shoved each other to get a better place in line, shouting at each other and even uttering foul words just to ensure that they would be able to kiss or at least touch the relic. He thought about the air full of miasma and the chest dripping with saliva being groped by the inhabitants who considered it sacred, and he knew that in a few weeks, if God did not intervene, most of them would be dead.

The exile pressed on and left the town. He had barely walked two hundred paces on the open road when he spotted a tiny lump in the middle of the road. He squinted, trying to make out what it was. He was about a yard away when he realized it was a little bird. Yes, a tiny bird. He touched the bird with the toe of his left boot and verified that the little sparrow was indeed dead. Perhaps the day before it had been flying, hopping from branch to branch, pecking at ripe fruit to nourish itself and delighting in its sweetness. Now it was just an inert little body that would soon be eaten up by ants and worms.

His gaze lingered on the bird a moment longer. Suddenly and most unexpectedly, the words of a teacher who had taught his divine doctrine centuries ago came to mind: Are not two sparrows sold for a small coin? Yet not one of them falls to the ground without your Father.

When the exile resumed his journey, his eyes were brimming with tears.

CHAPTER 11

"Oh! Excuse me! I beg your pardon!" exclaimed a man who had nearly knocked the exile to the ground.

The exile took a step to keep his balance and looked at the unexpected interlocutor. Instinctively, he put his hand on his belt to check if he still had his purse and calmed down when he realized it was still in place.

"You must excuse me," the man continued. "I was leaving the church right now, and my heart was more in heaven than on earth…"

The exile would have wished that however far away his heart was, he had kept his eyes on where he was going.

"It's fine. It's not important," he said as he tried to resume his walk.

"It is important. It really is, sir," continued the stranger. "Allow me at least treat you to a jug of wine."

"Sir, that's not necessary...," said the exile.

"I would be offended if you didn't accept," insisted the individual who had bumped into him.

The exile looked him over. The man was not dressed badly. Possibly, he could be a gentleman or at least an official in the service of the king, a bishop, or a nobleman. Who knew? What if he were someone of importance? He couldn't afford an altercation. Indeed, he couldn't. He tried to make his smile as friendly as possible.

"If that is so," he said politely, "I accept."

"Wonderful!" the man responded delightedly, slapping the exile on the shoulder. "Let's go to the Golden Rooster Inn."

The exile did not feel the slightest desire to accompany the man and began to think about how he could get rid of him as soon as possible. If he accepted one round from him and in turn treated him to another, he might be able to leave quietly.

The Golden Rooster Inn looked exactly like any of the hundreds of inns that were found in that country. Wooden tables, benches next to them, barrels piled up on top of each other, greedy-looking innkeepers, and stairs leading to the floor above with rooms for rent—that was, in essence, the panorama seen over and over again and were centers of infection that the exile sought to avoid.

"Innkeeper! Innkeeper!" the man shouted, gesticulating wildly. "A jug of wine! Make it red!"

"I like to go to church, sir," he said to the exile, resting his hands on the table. "Yes indeed, sir. It is very useful. By the most Blessed Mary, it is."

The arrival of the jug of wine obliged the man to be silent for a brief moment. With pompous ceremony he made a sign of the cross with the edge of his hand over the drink and moved his lips as if he were uttering a prayer. Then he grabbed the jug and poured wine into the two mugs in front of them. Next he brought the mug to his mouth and took a long, greedy drink before setting it down with a completely satisfied thunk.

"Ah! This red wine is good," he said, smacking his lips. "Very good."

The exile remained silent as he moistened his lips with the wine.

"As I was saying," the man continued, pouring himself more wine, "going to church not just on Sundays and holy days, but with frequency, is very good. For example, do you know the difference between a venial and a mortal sin?"

The exile nodded, indicating that he knew but didn't say anything. Instead, he settled himself in his seat, convinced he would have to patiently bear the exposition of theology that his host wanted to unload on him.

"Mortal sin," he said, raising the index finger of his right hand, "entails the agonies of hell if one dies without having confessed. Venial sin does not carry such serious consequences, but it does result in suffering in purgatory, which can last thousands of years. Now, the Church who is a Mother ... a Mother! ... has arranged for pious actions that can free us from the penalties of venial sin. For example, crossing yourself with holy water. Yes sir, crossing yourself with holy water. So, every time I pass by a church, I go in and make the sign of the cross. My venial sins are gone, and who knows if some mortal sin isn't gone with them..."

He underscored the last statement with a laugh, then lifted the mug to his mouth and emptied it. He smacked his lips again and looked at the exile with a merry expression in his eyes.

"I'm not saying that a person who has murdered, for example, does not deserve to go to hell, but there are sin, which even though they are sins, can only be classified as venial. For example, a little lie. A little white lie. I go home and my wife asks me, 'Where have you been?' Where have I been! And why does she care? I was where I wanted to be is what I think. Well, I will answer with what seems good to me, that I've been to Mass. And that's it. Yes sir, I know it's not quite right. It's a lie, but it is a venial sin. I'll give you another example. I am out in the countryside. Yes, I am out in the country and I am hungry. We are all hungry sometimes. Then I see that Uncle Jean's vineyard is a few steps away, just a few steps, and I say to myself, well, let's go eat some grapes. Is that going to ruin Uncle Jean? Of course not. So I go into his field and snag a cluster ... or two. Yes, it is not quite right, I know, but it is nothing more than a venial sin. A peccadillo. And Our Holy Mother, the Church, allows us to free ourselves from our punishment through some holy actions such as..."

"Crossing yourself," said the exile.

"Exactly!" the man smiled, taking another drink.

In conversations of this nature, they went through the first round and then a second, which the exile paid for, and a third that he could not avoid and a fourth that sheer courtesy deemed obligatory. Throughout it all, he kept his resolve to drink as little as possible while the man continued to fill his belly with a wine that, well, was not entirely bad.

"Your company is very agreeable, sir," said the exile, "but I must continue my journey. If you'll excuse me…"

"But, sir," exclaimed the pious wayfarer, "it is already getting dark. It's by no means sensible to continue on your way and be overtaken by the night. No, no, no. Not at all. Let me make you a proposition. You have made an excellent impression on me, and you're obviously an honest man. I would dare to say educated, yes, even cultured. You cannot risk a mishap by traveling at night. I will tell you what I have in mind. Allow me to treat you to dinner and then share my room with me at this inn. I have already paid for the rest of the week anyways."

"I can't accept that," said the exile while shaking his head. "I thank you from my heart, but I have to continue my journey and…"

"But, sir, it's almost dark. You will not reach the next town before everything is as black as pitch. Listen to me. Allow me to treat you to dinner and then share my room, which as I have already said, I have paid for in advance. I have to perform some act of charity to make up for my many sins, and you must not try to stop me."

The exile did not feel the slightest desire to continue in the company of the man, not only because his theology was deeply disagreeable to him but also because something inside told him he was not to be trusted.

He was thinking of what he could say to justify his immediate departure when the man got up and walked with a quick but unsteady step to find the innkeeper. He located him by a table at the end of the room and began talking to him. The exile could not hear what was said, but the innkeeper kept nodding his head as the man spoke to him and pointed in his direction.

Finally, the man politely bowed his head, and as the innkeeper obsequiously returned the gesture, he walked back to the exile.

"Problem solved," he said when he got to the table. "He will serve us dinner right now and then you can share my room. I hope you don't mind that I chose the menu, but since I am paying..."

"I cannot permit you...," the exile began, but the man put up his left hand to silence him.

Dinner was not bad. The choice of dishes was quite acceptable, and the exile had to admit that his dinner companion had good taste. He continued to endure the man's moral lessons with as much patience as he could muster and tried to eat quickly in order to be able to rest as soon as possible.

Preceded by one of the employees of the tavern, they went to the room where they were going to spend the night. The exile quickly noticed that one of the beds was smaller than the other, similar to the ones some officers use during military campaigns. Located by the door, the piece of furniture, if it deserved to be called that, gave the impression of being improvised and put there quickly at the last minute.

His host insisted on sleeping on that shabby cot, but the exile was unwilling to accept that. Only after facing staunch resistance from his companion was the exile compelled to give in and accept the only thing in the room that could somewhat properly be called a bed.

Still, the exile did not want to let his guard down. He decided to sleep with his clothes and boots on. That way, at least the money he had on him and in his boots would be safe. It was not the most comfortable way to spend the night, but he had slept in the open and in the countryside for several days so that even the hard and narrow bed seemed a delight. In fact, he had barely laid his head on the pillow when he fell fast asleep.

The exile woke up with a jolt when the cock crowed. The fowl seemed especially desperate because it strung together its crows one after another with an urgency meant to toss all the neighbors out of bed.

He blinked to shake off his sleep and turned his head to the left to see how his acquaintance from the day before was doing. Only his acquaintance wasn't there.

He sat up in one quick movement as he opened and closed his eyes to confirm what he already knew. The man had disappeared. The exile instantly grabbed his bags, which were by the head of the bed, but except for his books, there was nothing left inside. Clothes, money, food, all had disappeared as if carried off by a strong wind.

He jumped off the bed and began to pat himself. Yes, the money he had on him was still in place and so was the money he had hidden at the bottom of his boots. And maybe ... maybe he could still find the thief.

In one swift motion he threw the bags over his shoulder, opened the door, and rushed to the ground floor of the inn. He wanted to run as soon as he reached the street, but he never got there. He was a few steps away from the door when the innkeeper intercepted him.

"Your valet said when he left this morning that you would pay the bill."

The exile felt a rush of apprehension rise from the pit of his stomach to his throat.

"My valet?" he barely managed to get out.

"Yes, your valet," the innkeeper said pointedly as he crossed his arms. "The one who told me what you wanted to have for dinner yesterday. The one who asked us to put a more modest bed for him in your room. The one who left early this morning to prepare your accommodation in the next stop on your journey..."

Instantly, the exile understood the whole scam. The man had not treated him at all. In fact, he had drunk, dined, and slept at the exile's expense. When he had thought that the man was choosing the dishes with the innkeeper, the rogue was instead presenting himself as a diligent valet transmitting his master's orders. There was no denying he was a clever scoundrel.

"How much do I owe you?" he asked the innkeeper and had to contain his anger when he heard the amount. The owner of that unfortunate place was probably also defrauding him, but the extortion would have been impossible without the initial deception of the man who was so fond of crossing himself with holy water.

The exile reached for his belt and withdrew the sum stated by the innkeeper. It was unjust and not a small loss, but it would have been absurd to refuse to pay. Calling the constables, having the man arrested and brought before a judge was the last thing he wanted. Losing the money was indeed regrettable, but even more regrettable would be to be sidetracked from his journey, and he knew from experience that that was quite possible. He watched the innkeeper make a bow before him as if he were a duke and not in fact an exile. Then he walked out, knowing he would never have good memories of the place.

As he passed the church where he had met the swindler, almost without realizing what he was doing, he moved away from the building. Then he headed out of town. He had been walking in the open country for a while and reflecting on what had happened when suddenly a smile appeared on his face.

Certainly, the man had been a shameless scoundrel, a rogue, but one had to admit that he acted with ingenuity. How many had been tricked by that ruse? How many innkeepers had believed his lies, and how many pretended to swallow them, knowing that they could profit from the deception? How many would believe that empty talk about venial sins and how easily they could be erased? How many characters like him proliferated throughout the countrysides of Spain, France, and Germany, taking advantage of the innocence, superstition, or foolishness of the people?

And then the exile felt his face begin to quiver. But the quivering was not at all due to discomfort, illness, or fear. Rather, it was because all of a sudden the exile had discovered a laughable, outrageously comic side to what had happened. The quiver of his chin quickly gave way to laughter, a clean, sonorous, enjoyable laughter.

Then it got louder and more rollicking, bubbling up from the depths of his being. He had to stop walking because his mirth prevented him from going on. His hands went to his belly as his whole body shook. Before he knew it, he slid to the ground, his legs no longer able to withstand the force of his laughing.

All he could do at this point amidst the uncontrollable laughter was utter two words: venial sins!

CHAPTER 12

During the endless, monotonous weeks that followed, the exile did not stop or deviate from his journey north. He had adopted a general rule of stopping only at hamlets and farms where they would pay for his work with a bowl of soup and a night in the barn.

He would avoid the larger settlements, certain that nothing good could come from stopping in those places, even briefly, before reaching his destination. There was no doubt in his mind that corrupt mayors, rogues, and thieves, like those he had already encountered, were to be avoided.

Nor did he want to meet up with Fernando, Alfonso, and his brother. Until now he had seen them only one more time, but it had been at a distance. He might not be so lucky another time. He wondered where they could be at this point in their travels. Did they continued to travel ahead of him or had he overtaken them? Yes of course they could have given up the pursuit, but knowing them...

Thus, walking every day, he arrived at another farm, one more on a journey that had already lasted for weeks and could take many more months. It was one more house in a succession of rural enclaves that he had passed through and that stretched on and on over the days. It was nestled in a small meadow just like the hundreds he had come across since leaving his hometown.

It had a well where one could draw water, exactly like the ones he had drunk from daily along the way. Everything was the same. Even when he saw a couple of children playing not far from the entrance to the house, he did not think that they were any different from children in his own country or in the one he was now traversing. The only thing that was totally distinctive was the woman.

She came out of the small door of the house, drying her hands on an apron tied around her waist. Her hair was black, and she wore it pulled back. Her complexion was uncommonly white. White, but not reddish or pink like other peasant women he had seen. It was the white of coral or mother-of-pearl. Her oval-shaped face had beautiful, shapely eyebrows, black like her hair, with large dark eyes under their arcs. Her beauty was unique.

In fact, what most caught the exile's attention was the peculiar grace that emanated from her features. He had seen women with vitality, health, beauty, even sensuality before, especially in the countryside. But the best word to describe what this woman possessed was kindness. Yes, she had an exquisite kindness that seemed to descend from her hair to the soles of her feet, criss-crossing every inch of her body.

The woman became aware of the exile's presence, but her face did not exhibit the slightest fear, anxiety, or concern. Instead, just for an instant her eyebrows arched in a look that could have been one of questioning or surprise.

She did not move towards him. It was as if she were sending a message that if he wanted something, he would have to come to her.

So that's what he did, trying to ensure that each of his steps communicated tranquility, enough at least so that the woman would not feel uneasy.

"Good afternoon, ma'am," he said, bowing his head slightly. "I am passing through and I need a place to stay tonight. I can pay for a bowl of soup and for permission to sleep in your barn. That's all I need. Nothing else."

The woman looked at him for a moment. Then, she smiled unexpectedly, revealing dimples. The exile had seen that particular feature in other people, both men and women, but it seemed to him that on her face they were endowed with special beauty. Again, it was that peculiar gentleness that captivated him.

"Are you sure you will have enough with only one bowl of soup?" she said with her arresting smile.

The exile barely managed to mumble a few words of assent.

"You can wash with water from the well. I'll let you know when dinner is ready."

The woman reentered the house while the exile went to the well, threw the bucket to the bottom, and pulled it up full in order to wash up. He was drying his hands when he noticed that two children were looking at him.

The elder was a boy with hair as black as his mother's, though he had slightly darker skin. The girl, who looked three or four years younger, was lighter-skinned and her hair was also as black as a crow's wing.

The exile could not help but smile when he saw them. He thought to himself that they were wonderful children, and who knew what those two would become when they grew up? Anything, no doubt, but for the moment, they seemed like two slices of heaven fallen from above to illuminate with their innocent looks a world that was not.

"Hello," he said addressing the boy, "what's your name?"

The boy looked at him with a mixture of shyness and curiosity but remained silent.

"His name is Jacquot," replied his sister.

"Ah, Jacquot, well, well. And yours?"

"Su."

"Su? Very good. It's a nice name, like Jacquot. And Momma? Does your momma have a name, too?"

"Yes, of course. Her name is Marguerite," Jacquot replied.

"Marguerite," repeated the exile, "what about Papa?"

"No Papa," Su said.

"Papa is away on a trip," Jacquot put in.

The exile felt a sense of discomfort when he heard that the father of the family was not there. Perhaps it was true that he was absent, and perhaps that absence would only last a few days. Or perhaps the man had been taken to work in the fields of the local lord, to harvest in the bishop's lands, or to die fighting for the king. But whatever the task, he had been forced to leave behind a wife and two children. No one cared what might happen to them. The sound of a bell startled him from his thoughts.

"Dinnertime! Children, wash your hands!"

The exile lowered the bucket from the edge of the well and placed it within the reach of the two children, who soon were splashing water on each other, their play sprinkled with laughter.

He watched them head for the house, and only then did he start walking after them. He was a few steps from the door when the woman came out with a large bowl in her right hand and a small bowl in her left.

"Here's your soup. I have also given you some cheese and bread. I have no wine."

"That's all right," replied the exile. "I don't usually drink."

A look of relief passed over her face. It was gone quickly but not before he caught it. For whatever reason, it seemed as if she disliked men that drank, and he had just passed the first test.

He accepted the bowls and sat down on the ground by the threshold of the house. He took a sip of soup and felt unexpectedly happy. As the hot liquid reached his stomach, it filled him with an extraordinary feeling of a person who knows he is enjoying something apparently trivial, but which is in actuality brimming with goodness.

A light breeze rose, gently caressing his face and brushing the hair on the back of his hands. The sun had begun to set and as it descended it was not in a rush, but seemed more like a child putting off the inescapable moment when she had to leave a game and go indoors. Inside the house, he heard the muffled shouts of the children. It was probably in joy or protest over the food.

He thought to himself how curious it was that humans overlook the countless real pleasures of life. Kings send their armies to conquer a piece of land or subdue those who are foreign to them; clergymen tell lies in order to control the fearful or to extract money from the powerful; tax collectors are the minions who serve both. Yet how little they realize that the happiness we have been given to enjoy in this world sometimes appears in the form of a slice of cheese, a sip of fresh water, the aroma of the countryside, a few drops of rain, or a child's game.

Suddenly the exile felt a sharp, knife-like stab in his heart. While he was finishing his soup, a rapid succession of images passed through his mind: the fields around his home, the rooms in his house, the books that were lost, the shade of the vineyards, even snippets of the time when he and his brother were children, playing together and loving each other.

He realized that none of it had been enjoyed in its proper measure and that everything had disappeared, never to return, never to be experienced again. He tried to hold back pangs of regret that, like the hottest summer heat, were beginning to suffocate him. He felt alone, tired, but above all, small. He looked at the nearby mountains, and it seemed as if at any moment they could fall on him and crush him. He looked at the sky and felt that the clouds could unleash a downpour that would carry him away just as the wind sweeps away dry leaves. He stared at the ground and thought that at any moment it could open up and swallow him. His happiness, so real and tangible just a few moments before, had evaporated like dew at sunrise.

"Would you like some more bread?"

He shook his head as if waking from a dream and turned his gaze towards the voice. The woman's smile was in such stark contrast to the sensations that were tormenting him that for an instant, he felt another pang in his chest, but it dissipated as quickly as it had come. He jumped to his feet and said:

"Yes ma'am. Thank you."

The woman handed him the piece of bread. The exile took it with great care, but instead of eating it, he put it in the shoulder bag that was resting on the ground.

"Why don't you eat it now?" inquired the woman.

"Because right now I am satisfied," replied the exile. "Tomorrow..."

"Tomorrow, the Good Lord will also give you your daily bread. Eat the one I gave you today."

The exile fixed his gaze on the woman and, without taking his eyes off her, reached into the shoulder bag, took out the piece of bread, and put it in his mouth. He chewed it deliberately as if he wanted to enjoy every morsel.

"Do you come from afar?" asked the woman.

"Yes, from far away."

"Your manner of speaking..."

"I'm not from this kingdom, ma'am."

"No? But you speak my language very well..."

"Thank you so much, ma'am. You are very kind."

It seemed like a curtain was suddenly drawn across her face, hiding what was in her heart.

"I will show you where you can sleep," she said as she walked away.

The exile did not follow her. Rather, he chose to remain where he was so that he could contemplate the way the woman walked. Yes, she moved with the same elegance and grace he had observed in her gaze a short time before. He realized that it had to be a natural quality because it was clear this woman had not been educated. She had not come from a noble court, and she wasn't even the daughter of a wealthy personage who might have kept her cloistered and languishing in a house. Seeing the woman was like looking at a flower of exceptional beauty, like caressing a delicate pearl, or savoring a delicious fruit. The quality she had was natural and without guile.

"Are you not coming?" asked the woman who had reached the barn and discovered that the exile was still in the same place.

"Yes, forgive me," replied the exile as he hurried to her.

"See," she said, indicating with her right hand, "The animals are down here. They have no reason to bother you, but one never knows.... If you go to the upper part, you will be more comfortable. There is also straw to help you sleep better. And oh, I beg you not to relieve yourself indoors. It leaves a bad odor..."

The exile noticed that the woman, unlike other peasant women who expressed themselves with crude frankness, had blushed a little on giving him these instructions. Where could this woman have come from?

"Yes ma'am. I will do so."

"If you get thirsty..."

"I will go to the well."

"I can leave you a jug..."

"Please don't bother, ma'am. I will go to the well."

"All right. If you don't need anything else, I will leave you alone."

"God keep watch over you, ma'am."

The woman inclined her head slightly in acknowledgement and started back to the house. She had barely taken a few steps when the exile called out to her:

"Ma'am...," he began.

The woman turned without a word.

"Thank you very much," the exile stammered, "thank you so very much. You are very kind."

"Get some rest," said the woman as she resumed her walk back to the house.

The exile went into the barn, climbed the ladder to the upper portion, set his bags on the floor, and made a pile of straw to sleep on. He smelled the pungent odor of the animals, heard the whistling of the wind as it filtered in through the joints of the building, and felt the warmth of clean, freshly cut straw.

As he gently fell asleep, memories of other happier times came to him in sweet waves.

CHAPTER 13

The exile had planned on spending only two or at the most three or four days on the farm, but the days somehow flew by and before he knew it, he had been there a month.

He repaired doors and fences, harvested and stored, whitewashed and pruned. Then Jacquot fell ill with one of those ailments that seem to arise for the express purpose of cutting short the lives of children, but the exile attacked the illness like a highwayman. For two weeks the child was on the verge of death, while the same was denied his worried mother, and then he recovered as if nothing had happened to him.

By then the exile had been busy making toys for Su and had taught the convalescent Jacquot how to play checkers on a board he cobbled together and painted in his spare time. All of this he had done under the quiet gaze of the woman.

Only once did the distance they maintained between them disappear. It was precisely the day that Jacquot turned the corner on his illness. The exile gazed with joy at the boy's improvement and instinctively grabbed Marguerite's hand next to him. It was only for an instant, but the woman returned the gesture, squeezing his hand even more tightly. The exile felt the gratitude, the beauty and the warmth from her hand, but he released it immediately as if it had burned him. Yet it hadn't burned him. He had simply felt something so beautiful that he had no words to describe it.

One day Marguerite found him reading after dinner and asked what the book was about. He began to tell her and was surprised to hear her ask with utmost respect that he help her become a participant in that written world.

Thus a bond formed between them that he had never enjoyed with any woman, not even in his years as a student. He began to wait for the end of each workday, for the woman to find him, and for the two of them to enjoy the words flowing from pages that had been printed in the same city he was trying to reach.

Little by little, each gesture, each expression, each moment took on a special meaning. The jug of water that Marguerite brought him, the piece of bread she handed to him, the smile that she gave him, the attention she paid him while he read, all became little bursts of joy that flowed over the battered soul of the exile.

One day, he realized that this woman was indeed a balm to him. Yes, she was a feminine salve that covered his past and present wounds. Suddenly, none of those wounds seemed to have any relevance and if they remained ... they were greatly diminished, as if they hardly existed. Those days—it was a right and a good thing to thank God for them—were truly healing him.

Nevertheless, the exile could not and did not want to deceive himself. To stay there was impossible. Absolutely impossible. At some point or another, they might find him; it was even plausible that his three pursuers would be the ones to do so.

But even if this were a totally isolated place, even if the Holy Office never reached this meadow, even if ... no. He could never stay there. He was well aware of what he had to do and that he had to reach his destination.

Consequently, one evening after he and Marguerite had laughed together while playing with the children, the exile told her that he would be leaving the following day.

A curtain immediately seemed to close over Marguerite's face. It was as if her features were paralyzed, and an almost opaque color spread over them and blurred them. Her lips parted slightly, but no sound came out.

"I will be leaving before sunrise ... to make the most of the day," explained the exile.

"Stop by the house before you leave, and I'll give you some food for the trip."

"I had better get it today ... so that tomorrow you won't have to get up early because of me."

They both knew that the exile said this because he didn't want any farewells, but neither of them said anything.

"And the children?" Marguerite asked.

"Tomorrow," the exile replied, "you can tell them tomorrow... whatever you think is best. Let them enjoy today."

Certainly the children continued to have fun, but a heavy mantle of silence fell over Marguerite and the exile.

When it was time to go to sleep and he had accepted the food she brought to him at the barn door, he could barely articulate a few words of gratitude, which she received with visible discomfort. He watched her retreat to the house with the little ones, and he thought how not even sorrow had deprived her walk of the grace that characterized it.

He spent a restless night. A hundred times he tried to sleep, and a hundred times he woke up gripped by anxiety. It was as if the innumerable discomforts of the barn had conspired to prevent him from getting a single hour of rest.

Finally, worn out by the effort of trying to sleep, he dozed lightly. He could not tell how long he remained in that state, but he would never forget the moment he woke up. With a start he noticed a yellow light resting on the floor a few steps away. Next to it he saw outlined the figure of Marguerite. She wore a white blouse that left her arms bare and a dark skirt he had seen her wear many times. Instantly the exile sat and then stood up.

"I thought you were about to leave and ... and I wondered if you wanted to hug me goodbye."

In his heart, the exile felt a warning that if he agreed to the request, he would be opening the door to a force he perhaps could not contain. The warning was clear, strong, almost imperious, but before he could stop himself, so he opened his arms and enfolded Marguerite in an embrace.

He did not have words to express the ocean of voluptuous sensations that ran through his entire being, from the depths of his soul to the farthest recesses of his body. It was as if Marguerite's kindness, sweetness, and beauty had dissolved and become fluid, permeating his entire being and cleansing him of any impurity he might harbor.

"I'm going to kiss you," he heard himself say as his lips sought Marguerite's. It was a long, intense, deep kiss. He felt her tremble and let out a muffled moan.

He pulled away and saw Marguerite lower her eyes in shy modesty. He caressed her cheek and was surprised at its softness. How could she possibly have that complexion after spending time in the sun? How could her arms be like warm alabaster? How was it possible that Marguerite had evoked in him what no one had ever evoked before?

He wished he had stopped there, but he did not. He caressed her ears and lips; ran his fingers down her back and arms; let his hands graze over her face and neck, but he was careful not to lower his hands below the waist or to brush against her breasts. It was as if he wanted to absorb her beauty with his fingertips, but without making a single movement that could cause her offense.

He knew then, knew it with complete certainty, that she was ready to give herself to him; that she would hardly be able to put up any resistance; and that if she tried, she would still give in because every inch of her being cried out with a desire to be one with him. He knew it and he also knew he could not accept that gift. Receiving it would have been like stealing. A robbery not out of necessity but one that was selfish, tainted, unkind. It would have meant taking the woman without any assurance that he would see her again, that he could give her more than just the kisses of that one night, that he would be more than a fleeting comfort to her in the loneliness of months or perhaps years to come.

Gently pulling her away from him, he ran his fingers slowly and gently over Marguerite's left ear and cheek. He kissed her, this time on the forehead, as he would have done with a beloved child.

"I must go," he said in the gentlest tone he could.

"Will you come back?" she asked in the same voice a child would use to ask her mother if she will return.

"I don't know," he confessed and saw how sorrow clouded Marguerite's delicate face.

He took a deep breath, stroked her face, and said: "It is true. I really don't know. Only God knows."

He was about to tell her that he would return for her one day, that the wait would come to an end, that at some point in the future they would be united and would never part again. But he did not say any of that because he was the first to admit he had no guarantee of reaching even the end of the day alive. The Holy Office could catch him at any bend in the road, and his life could end at the stake. What guarantee could he give a woman, especially her, under those conditions?

"Go back," he said, "the children could wake up, and they would be frightened if they didn't see you."

Marguerite threw herself against the exile's chest and hugged him tightly as if she wanted to stay there forever. The exile let her remain there for a few moments, then gently pushed her away.

"Go on," he insisted.

Marguerite nodded in assent, then turned and walked towards the ladder. The exile did not see her. He had closed his eyes, certain that if he looked at her again his resolve would break. Only when he heard her steps recede towards the house did he reopen them.

CHAPTER 14

He observed the town. He would have gladly gone around it, but it just wasn't doable. He should have taken a detour a few hours earlier, but now it was too late and it didn't seem sensible to retrace his steps.

He decided to eat while thinking of an alternative. He moved off the road, sat under a tree, and leaned his back against the trunk as if it were the back of a chair. It wasn't bad. He opened the shoulder bag and took out a piece of cheese. It was all he had left of the food Marguerite had given him. Marguerite ... how was she? How were the children? Did Su continue to play with the toys he had made for her? Was Jacquot still healthy?

He waved his hand in front of his forehead as if scaring off a fly, but he was, in reality, trying to shoo away thoughts that could become painful.

It was then that he noticed an elderly man who was heading towards the town. He was leaning on a cane, and it was obvious that he needed it because one of his knees was badly damaged. He couldn't determine the exact nature of the man's infirmity without examining it, but yes, the kneecap could no longer be what it was when he was born. Observing the impaired limb, he remembered, by one of those associations of ideas that so often happens in the human mind, another person who suffered from a similar ailment: Alfonso, one of his pursuers.

The first time he had heard of him had been through a mutual acquaintance. The man had liked something he had read that was written by Alfonso. He lacked formal education, and the exile was not surprised to discover after attentive reading that Alfonso's work was nothing more than a mediocre, easily forgotten text.

For years, he did not hear any more about Alfonso until one day someone told him that he had vigorously defended one of the worst steps taken by the country's rulers. The measure taken by the authorities was, in the exile's opinion, profoundly detrimental. The king, in point of fact, had decided that the subjects of the kingdom could not study at any foreign university in order to avoid being corrupted by heresies. Apparently, the students' faith was so fragile that simply hearing something different could sever them from the church they belonged to. Or perhaps—and this was the most probable reason—the beliefs of that church could only be sustained by burnings at the stake, ignorance, and superstition and could not endure the comparison with points of view that differed from the ones the church imposed with blood and fire.

Thanks to that royal decree, generation after generation of students would be doomed to never learning about new discoveries and inventions in the rest of the world. But of course, the clergy would sleep in peace, and the king would surely feel that he was closer to God. Among the defenders of this unjust and, above all, foolish measure was Alfonso.

The exile had not expressed his point of view at the time, but one day he learned that Alfonso had begun to spread slander against him; slander that could create serious complications and even land him in a dungeon of the Holy Office. The exile had never fully understood why he had done so. Perhaps it was due to an overabundance of zeal to close the country, like sealing off a room. Perhaps it was due to pure personal ambition, and so he had placed himself under the sun that warmed the most. Perhaps, it was that he liked to side with what was decided and imposed, fairly or unfairly, from above. Or perhaps it was just from pure envy.

As he thought about it, it was curious how similar his attitude was to Fernando's. Yes, Alfonso was somewhat better educated, but the exile did not think that what he harbored deep in his heart was any better. No, it certainly wasn't. Then he smiled. Perhaps, after all, he was not fleeing the kingdom because of the desire for orthodoxy on the part of some, but because of mere envy. That sometimes yellow, sometimes green, and sometimes black rot oozing from the hearts of the mediocre who hate the good fortune of others was perhaps the real reason he had to travel at night and in isolated places.

Seen in this way, maybe examining the history of humanity in the light of envy would be a healthy and instructive exercise. Undoubtedly the first murder, that of Abel at the hands of his brother Cain, had taken place because Cain envied his brother. Caesar had not been stabbed to death for the love of freedom, but because of the envy of those who could not abide someone who was brave, brilliant, and in a word, a genius. And surely Jesus was crucified because the religious leaders of his time envied the way multitudes followed him, people whose spiritual poverty had not been addressed by the temple authorities.

But ... what difference did it make? Alfonso was just one of many envious people who suddenly, rightly or wrongly, think they see someone better than themselves and instead of imitating them, admiring them, learning from their example, or even trying to surpass them, they decide instead to destroy them. They are like the snake that wanted to devour a firefly, and when the tiny animal asked the reptile why, it replied with only three words: because you shine. Yes, those individuals, no less vile than a viper, had decided to help take his life because they thought that he shone.

He stood up and decided to head towards the town. He would traverse it as quickly as possible and continue on his way as long as he could before nightfall. No guards were at the entrance, which he interpreted to mean that one did not have to pay a toll. And so it was. He continued down the street that twisted and turned before him, went up a slight incline, and arrived at the town square. At that point, he must have been about halfway through the town.

Then he saw some children yelling as they scampered about. But they were not playing. No. They were throwing filth at a man tied to a whipping post, the stone post found in villages where people convicted of certain crimes were tied. The unfortunate man had his hands tied with chains above his head, and since he was unable to protect his face, he turned his head, trying to hide it under his arm.

The exile thought it was a shameful spectacle. Even if somehow it were acceptable to expose someone to public shame, it was utterly disgraceful to leave them at the mercy of ignorant and cruel children and of no less cruel and ignorant adults, full of even worse passions.

He should have continued on his way without stopping, but he couldn't help going to the man. He chased away the children who were tormenting the wretch and stood looking at him for a moment.

At another time, his clothes might have been good, even elegant, but now they were nothing more than a smelly mix of all kinds of filth. Gobs of spit and excrement, rotting fruits and putrefied vegetables, dirt and liquids that he did not wish to identify had been thrown at him. The sign hanging on the post denounced him as a thief, and the exile thought he must have stolen a lot to be punished like this. Then, coughing, crying, spitting, the chained man lifted his head from under his arm.

The exile blinked in disbelief at the now exposed face. Yes, yes, it was him! He took a few steps closer to the criminal to dispel any doubts. Of course it was him! The chained man's eyebrows shot up as he also recognized the exile. He shifted in shame and put his face back under his arm.

The exile did not say a single word. He looked around for a fountain and discovered it a few steps away. He walked over to it, and taking his gourd he filled it completely. Then he took one of his shirts out of the shoulder bag and soaked it with water and returned to the post.

It was hard to get the man's head out from under his arm. He probably expected a blow so he resisted, but having both hands chained did not allow him to mount an effective resistance.

When the exile had his head in his hands, he grabbed onto his chin and began to clean the man's face with his water-soaked shirt. Initially, the thief tried to turn away, but realizing that the exile was only trying to help him, he let him take off the layer of dirt from his face. When the cleaning was done, the exile unstoppered the gourd and brought it to the man's lips. The man drank greedily, as if his life depended on it, and the exile figured he probably hadn't had a drop for several days.

"Drink slowly," he said, "or it can cause you harm."

But the chained man did not listen to him. His lips were parched like worn leather, and his throat burned. He didn't care in the least if he died as long as he could quench his thirst. He finished his very long drink with a cough. Then he looked down again.

"I have a feeling that this water has been more useful to you than the water you used to remove venial sins."

The man tried to hide his face deeper under his arm, and it seemed to the exile that he was holding back a sob.

"When you leave here, look for the true water of life and improve your theology, which, I am afraid, is what has gotten you here."

The exile picked up the shirt and the gourd and went back to the fountain. He washed the garment as best he could, wrung it out and spread it out to dry just a little, and then filled his bottle gourd up again.

He picked up the shirt and shook it. It was still wet but no longer dripping. He put it under his left arm and secured the gourd filled with water.

Before leaving, he looked back at the man who had swindled him not long ago. His face, now clean, was convulsed in sobs.

CHAPTER 15

For the first time since he left home, the exile felt he was unwelcome. In the previous weeks, he might have been viewed with curiosity, as quarry of the Holy Office, as a dupe for a scam, or as an object of love and desire, but at no time had he sensed outright hostility. Now he felt it all around. He had sensed it as soon as he arrived at the city.

Elsewhere, outsiders, strangers, and exiles like him were isolated individuals. One here, another there, maybe a family. However, this city was like a magnet that attracted all those who fled from intolerance, liberticide, and the Holy Office. And that powerful attraction had spread all over the continent.

In order to gain entrance to the city, one had to wait in a colossal line where one could hear French, German, Italian, Spanish, and countless other languages the exile did not recognize. Getting in the city meant, maybe, just maybe, escaping confiscation, imprisonment, death.

However, along with the possibility of refuge, welcome, and asylum, the city was full of natives who looked at the newcomers with suspicion. He grasped that perfectly when he saw how the people leaving the city looked with displeasure and even irritation at the line where the exile was waiting. It was obvious that the idea of receiving thousands of exiles—would there be the same large amount of people every day waiting to enter the city?—caused a mixture of anxiety, uneasiness, and hostility.

He had to wait several hours before he reached the entrance to the city. Finally, he found himself in front of a clerk who addressed him in French. The exile knew the language well, and he had been speaking it continually in recent months, so he answered with ease the questions about himself, his origin, and his reasons for coming to the city.

"Do not expect," said the clerk with a stern look, "to live here by begging. In this city, we strictly adhere to the teaching of Saint Paul the Apostle who said that those who do not work should not eat."

"It seems fair to me," replied the exile sincerely.

"Good, well … and what do you do?"

"I'm a physician."

The clerk stroked his beard thoughtfully. Then he looked at the exile and asked:

"Do you have the necessary instruments with you?"

"They were stolen from me weeks ago," the exile replied sadly.

"Don't worry. It happens often. The roads are unsafe and especially so for foreigners. We will take care of that. You must go to the Bourse Française. There they will try to give you proper instruments so that you can practice your profession. The guard here will tell you how to get there."

"Thank you very much, sir," said the exile with a respectful bow.

"Wait," said the clerk, "you will need this."

He scribbled a few lines on a piece of paper and handed it to the exile. Taking it from him he saw that it had his personal information and stated in big letters that he was a doctor. The exile thanked him again and then approached the guard who carefully instructed him on how to get to the Bourse.

The place in question was not far away. It was attached to a church and before it, as expected, stretched another line in which he recognized some of those who had preceded him at the entrance to the city. Most of them were artisans, perhaps some day laborers, but, in all cases, these were people used to making their own living. All their lives they had earned a living with hard work, and one would assume that they would do the same in this land, so far from where they had been born.

To pass the time as he waited, the exile took out one of his books from his shoulder bag and began to read. Thus occupied, he hardly noticed the time go by. In fact, he was so engrossed in his reading that he was surprised to find he was already at the table where they attended to the people. Instinctively, he held out the piece of paper that the clerk at the entrance to the city had given him. The person sitting before him took it and read it.

"Are you a doctor?" he asked as looked into his eyes.

"Yes, sir, I am," replied the exile.

"You will have, therefore, no objections to another doctor evaluating your knowledge..."

"No, none at all," replied the exile.

"Good. Wait over there please."

The exile could not help but smile as he thought how he was spending the whole day waiting. He again took a book out of his shoulder bag and started to read. A friendly, masculine voice brought him out of that pleasant pastime.

"Are you the doctor?"

The person who addressed him was a thin man with a white, pointy goatee and an almost completely bald head. He was dressed in all in black, although his neck was ringed by a thin, immaculately white ruffle, causing an almost luminous contrast of colors.

"Yes sir, I am."

"Well, I am obliged to give you some warnings. In this city, we most certainly help those in need in a Christian spirit, but we do not provide for idlers. We do not give alms, but we do help people as much as possible so that they can earn a living with their own efforts. If someone has a trade, we help them to practice it; if they don't, we try to teach them one so they can support themselves with the honest work of their hands. Do you understand me?"

"Yes, sir, I do."

"Perfect. In the event that a person has a trade or, as in your case, a profession, we can provide them with the appropriate instruments if they do not have them. I see that you do not have the essential instruments of a doctor."

"They were stolen from me when…"

The man with the little pointy beard raised his hand to stop him.

"We will perhaps have time later to go into details. The fact is that at present you don't have any. The instruments of a doctor are not cheap. It is not the same as giving tools to a shoemaker or a carpenter. The city is more than willing to help you, but it must make sure that you are a doctor and not an impostor who will get hold of the instruments and then run off to sell them elsewhere. Do you understand?"

The exile closed his eyes and nodded. Everything the man said was reasonable, but sadly it also made clear how woeful his situation was. In another time, in another place, he had been a respectable man, so respectable, in fact, that it aroused envy, as he well knew. Here and now, he was just an exile who had to submit to an exam as if he were back working on his baccalaureate.

"I understand you, yes. You can ask whatever you wish."

"I will do so," said the man with the goatee.

What followed was an exam of increasing difficulty. The first questions had to do with elementary concepts of anatomy. The exile did not know the terminology in French very well, but he circumvented the problem by giving the names of the organs in Latin, something that elicited more than one admiring comment from the examiner.

When the man was satisfied with this part, he went on to ask about specific diseases and ailments. All of them the exile knew well and had even treated. However, at a certain point the man with the goatee was no longer examining him but had started comparing his views on certain therapies with those of the exile. Without realizing it, he had stopped considering him an examinee and began to regard him as a seasoned colleague.

"And did it work?" he asked with great interest at one point in the conversation.

"Yes, very quickly. And thoroughly."

The examiner tugged on his goatee, and then ran his hands over his mustache and mouth. It was obvious that the man before him was no impostor, or a simple student of medicine, or even an inexperienced doctor. The man was indeed a remarkably competent professional.

"Please pardon me for this examination," he said at last. "I am truly sorry to have submitted you to a tiresome test, but we have no other way of assessing the truthfulness of what a new-comer claims. But I must tell you that I have no doubt you are an accomplished doctor."

Rather than a surge of joy upon hearing those words, the exile felt a stab of concern in his breast. This man had realized who he was, yes, but what if he now behaved like the people in his home country? What if, instead of accepting him, he now decided to cause him harm out of envy? What if, as was common in the kingdom where he had first seen light, being exceptional meant a straight path to the worst of misfortunes, not to recognition? What if this city that he had dreamed so much about was, in the end, full of people like Alfonso or Fernando?

"This city needs people like you," said the man with the sharp goatee, as if he had guessed the thoughts of the exile. "It is not that we do not need ropemakers or butchers, but someone like you … someone like you is a gift from heaven. You are the kind of person we need."

When he heard that, the exile felt as if something in his chest broke open, and emotion rose up through his throat and to his eyes, filling them with tears. Was this really possible?

"Come, come," said the man with the goatee, looking away so as not to embarrass the exile. "Don't worry. You are safe and here you will begin a new life. That life will not only be good for you but also for all who come to you."

The exile was unable to respond. The lump in his throat prevented him from speaking.

"Do you have a wife? Children? The city offers free schooling that is open for everyone. It is unusual, I know, but we are convinced that it is impossible to make progress in life without education. Indeed, it is even impossible to be a good Christian without knowing how to read and write. How can anyone study the Bible if they are illiterate?"

The exile had to work hard to keep his voice from cracking when he responded.

"No ... I don't have a wife. Nor children. I am alone."

"Being alone is better for escaping, but now that you are safe ... well, only God knows. I will issue an order that you be given the necessary equipment so that you can practice your profession. You will need accommodations, and a place to see patients..."

Again, the man tugged gently on his beard. It was obvious that he was deliberating something important.

"I know," he began finally, "that it is well below your possibilities, but would you accept staying in my house until you find a better place? It is a humble home, but it is clean and there you could begin to see your first patients..."

The exile knew now that he had started a new life.

CHAPTER 16

During the following weeks, the exile discovered that he was living in a very different world from the one he had known throughout his life. He had certainly hoped not to be pursued to this place. He had also thought that he could make some kind of a living.

However, he never expected he would see a place where there were no beggars for the simple reason that the Pauline principle of "whoever does not want to work should not eat" was practiced. He never expected to see a place where the children all went to school and, furthermore, did so because education was considered to be one of the first steps towards holiness. He never expected to see a place where the best were not persecuted out of envy, but promoted based on their worth. He never expected to see a place where lies and theft were not considered venial sins, but very serious transgressions against others. Even less did he expect to find expressions of art that focused on music, literature, and painting but that rejected the forging of creations that people bowed down to as if they were living beings instead of pieces of wood, metal, or plaster.

He had never thought of any of these things. He had aspired only to breathe easier, to not have to look back to see if he was being chased, and to not have to hide to avoid becoming a victim of the envious. Now he found himself thinking more and more that for all that to happen it was necessary for the population to live as these people did. If that were the case, the kingdom from which he had escaped could have been the richest in the world by now, but it was on its way to grinding poverty and appalling ruin, something that, because of its immense pride and closed-minded bigotry, it might never understand.

Yes, the exile thought to himself, it's true that in this life we are all foreigners and pilgrims, but there are places on earth that can make exile more agreeable, or at least more tolerable.

Without realizing it, the exile was recovering the feeling of pleasure that can only come from practicing a profession that one knows in depth and that is useful to others. Childhood illnesses, ailments of the elderly, women's maladies, the infirmities of men were issues that the exile resolved day after day with the same dedication and enjoyment as a mathematician who finds a clear solution to a complex problem. The swollen necks, broken limbs, and congested chests presented challenges that when properly treated translated into health and freedom for the patients.

It was precisely at those times when a fever dropped, when limbs moved again, when the pain disappeared, that images of happy times in the past filled the exile's mind. The time in his life when his mother insisted on feeding him and his brother at all hours; when his brother didn't pursue him but laughed with him; when he began to savor the pleasure of reading, when he realized he could discover for himself a multitude of things he had never been taught and would never be taught. All this had been beautiful, even very beautiful, but those times were gone just like ripe grapes eaten in autumns past or buds on trees in springtimes long ago.

Now, when these memories came to mind, they did not cause him any pain, but became sweet remembrances of the past that the present had helped him overcome. In this unfamiliar and unexpected life he was living, he understood that a new and better world than the one he had known was possible. It was a world where it was even possible to be happy, and happy in an entirely different way.

Little by little, the life of the exile was acquiring the characteristics of normality. He ate without looking over his shoulder to ward off a threat, slept without thinking about continuing his flight, walked without looking out of the corner of his eye at anyone who appeared on the road, read without having to hide from informers, worked without having to guard against the envious. He even allowed himself to enjoy small pleasures.

More to please the doctor with the goatee than for his own enjoyment, the exile played a game of chess with him almost every night. He had never mastered the game, and even if he had, he would have let his host win. He was a good man, a hard worker and a lover of his profession and of books. He was a widower and had two children, but they did not live with him anymore. The household chores were done by a housekeeper who arrived before dawn and left a little before sunset. It was not surprising that this doctor, older than himself and alone, was pleased to talk with a colleague from a distant kingdom.

One afternoon, the exile decided to take a walk outside the city. He was already relatively well known, and when he walked in the street, people greeted him and even approached him to ask him questions or make comments. The exile was not a vain person, but he appreciated those displays of affection because they confirmed to him that he was putting down roots in that new cosmos.

With that feeling of satisfaction, he kept walking and without realizing it, he found himself walking under the trees that cast their shadows outside of the city. It had rained and the exile enjoyed the smell of wet earth and the sparkle of water on tree leaves.

He was smiling with pleasure as he enjoyed those small gifts when he heard a snap behind him. Instinctively, he turned towards the unexpected noise. But he didn't have a chance to see anything.

Before he could turn all the way, he felt a sharp blow to the crown of his head. He barely felt the pain because suddenly everything went black and the world vanished.

CHAPTER 17

When he came to, the exile felt that his entire body had been reduced to a convulsing painful mass. The crown of his head stung terribly, as if a torch had lit his head on fire.

He tried to move and touch that point of torment, but he realized then that his hands were tied behind his back. His movements not only sent currents of pain from his wrists to his neck, but the painful sensation also ran down his spine to his waist. He tried to move his feet but discovered that they, too, were tied, and attempting to move anything from the ankles to the waist caused a shock of intense pain in the knees.

He had been tied to a tree, and his body, which must have been in that position for hours, had become a kind of silent enemy, torturing him with unremitting waves of anguish. Then he tried to open his mouth, but realized that he had a gag in it that prevented him from speaking. Finally, little by little, he opened his eyes a crack.

With a heavy heart he spotted three men whom he knew very well just a few paces away. Yes, it was Fernando, Alfonso, and his own brother. They had found and kidnapped him precisely when he had already reached the place of refuge he had so yearned for and was enjoying a new, happy, and productive life. He had thought he was safe and it seemed that it was not so.

A feeling of immense grief washed over the exile. So in the end he was not to escape the dungeon, torture, or burning at the stake? And was it to be because of two envious people, one of whom he had fed for years and a third who shared his blood? He closed his eyes and tried to calm down. He knew that anger, anxiety, and fear are terrible companions, and in a bad situation they could be even worse than that.

The exile understood that he urgently needed to know what their plans were, what route they would take, and whether or not they had more people to help them. He also realized that the fact that they had seized him did not mean he could not escape. Falling into the hands of the Holy Office in the kingdom where he had been born amounted to a clear death sentence, but the truth was that they were not in that kingdom. Not yet. Not for days or weeks. An unexpected kick yanked him out of his reflections.

"Wake up, heretic," Fernando said in a harsh voice.

The kick from the round-faced pursuer had struck his left ankle, and the sharp pain forced him to clench his teeth to suppress a howl of pain.

"He won't wake up," Fernando said to his companions. "Maybe I'll have to kick him higher."

"That's enough," said another voice, which he recognized as his brother's.

Fernando's expression revealed his displeasure. There was no doubt he would have liked to kick him freely. Perhaps he thought he deserved to kick the exile for every plate of food he and his family had received from him.

The exile's brother pushed Fernando aside and leaned over his face.

"If I remove the gag, do you promise not to cry out?"

The exile nodded his head in assent, and his brother removed the handkerchief from around his head and then removed the rag they had stuffed in his mouth. The exile moved his tongue and eagerly inhaled the fresh air entering into his dry and bitter-tasting mouth.

"Do you want some water?" his brother asked.

He nodded again. His brother turned from the tree and took a few steps to a get a bottle gourd. He returned, leaned over the exile, and held the container to his parched lips. He drank avidly until his brother removed the gourd.

"I don't know if it is worth wasting water on him. I mean...," Fernando muttered.

"The way back is not short," said the brother. "Are you proposing that we deliver the corpse of a man who died from thirst to the Holy Office?"

Fernando lowered his forehead in a gesture so characteristic of him that resembled the movements of an ox.

"No, of course not," intervened Alfonso, who until that moment had been silent. "He has to arrive very alive, and then he will answer for all his crimes."

The exile was more curious than indignant at the word "crimes." What was the knave referring to? Did he consider it a crime to disagree with a policy that forbid students in the kingdom from going to foreign universities? Did he think that abiding by what the Bible said with regard to theology was also a crime? Was it a crime to be better than the mediocre and the envious? He asked himself all this but said nothing, knowing that he had already been condemned by that servile individual before the Holy Office had even rendered a judgment.

"That is true, Alfonso," Fernando said, "but since we have him here, I don't know if it is worth dragging him to his fate. A rope with knots will..."

"We are not outlaws," the brother interrupted, "nor executioners. Everything will be carried out according to the law."

"But there's still a problem," said Fernando. "We only have three horses..."

"You will give him yours," the brother cut in.

Fernando raised his bovine forehead in poorly contained anger. It was obvious that he did not agree at all with what he had just heard, but he didn't dare object.

"We can't pull this man tied behind a horse. We would attract attention, and it is quite possible that the authorities would force us to release him. It's even possible that we would be brought before a judge and in truth we have no jurisdiction in this kingdom..."

"Well, they would prove to be very bad Christians if they did try to obstruct the justice of the Holy Office," said Fernando angrily. "The divine Judge would surely give them their due punishment."

"No doubt, but for now we have to be careful. He has an undeniable look of a gentleman, which he is by the way, although he is also a heretic. You, on the hand, look like a villain, which is what you are after all. It is appropriate, therefore, that you go on foot and he on horseback."

Again, Fernando's face revealed the unpleasant impact these words had on him. No matter how one looked at it, the idea that he, who was in service of the Holy Office, had to agree to go on foot so that a heretic could go on horseback went against his most basic sense of decorum and religion. It was unfair and also immoral. It might even be close to heresy, but the time had not yet come to assert himself.

"I'll do as you say," said Fernando, lowering his head again, "but when we cross the border of the kingdom, he, a heretic, will go on foot and I will ride."

Fernando had hoped that one or more of his companions would support his statement, but Alfonso made as if he had not heard him, and the brother didn't say anything either.

"We could be back in less than a month," Alfonso said, changing the subject.

"It doesn't seem possible," Fernando mumbled.

"When we came, we lost a lot of time going back and forth, investigating, asking," Alfonso continued without hearing Fernando. "Now we will return almost in a straight line. We will only stop to give our horses and this fellow some rest."

Fernando caught the contemptuous tone with which Alfonso had referred to him and narrowed his eyes, as if this could lessen his humiliation, which felt like fire searing his skin.

"The first thing is to get away from the city as soon as we can," Alfonso continued. "If by any chance they notice his absence they could come looking for him..."

"Do you think so?" the brother interrupted him. "I don't think he's that important..."

"Of course he's not," Alfonso agreed, "but heretics protect each other. We can't rule out the possibility that they might try to rescue him."

"If that happens, I will cut his throat before they can even get close to him," said Fernando with angry determination.

"That's a good plan," Alfonso agreed. "We cannot tolerate the heretics saving him from his just punishment. And now we should get some rest and leave at dawn."

Fernando and the brother agreed and made ready to go to sleep. The exile saw that he would not be allowed to relieve himself or be untied. He would have to settle in and spend the night as best he could, despite the pain gripping most of his joints. He wished he could think of a way to escape the determined threesome guarding him, but realized that this was not the time. Now it was better to try to get a little rest. The following day he would have time to think of the best way to escape his predicament.

CHAPTER 18

The exile thought it was ironic that he was making the return journey towards death more comfortably than the journey that had distanced him, even if temporarily, from it. As his captors had determined the night before, he was mounted on one of the horses, although his hands were still tied, and Fernando never left his side. If he had tried to spur his mount or even move away a little, they would have caught him and most assuredly Fernando would have killed him.

During the past weeks, he had often thought about the reasons why Alfonso and Fernando had decided to come in pursuit of him. But now he realized that he had not stopped to think about what could have motivated his very own brother.

Of course, his case could be similar to that of Juan Díaz, who was murdered by his brother who considered him a heretic. However, the person who now rode alongside Alfonso had never been especially religious. Unless he had acquired unexpected religious fervor, which the exile had not heard about, that motive could be ruled out.

So then, what could have been the reason? That he had been his mother's favorite? In childhood, his brother had been the favorite of his father, who had always been closer to him and seen him as more like him. The inheritance? The exile could have received more from his father, but he rejected it precisely to prevent it from driving a wedge between them. Furthermore, his brother's life had always been safer and calmer than his, which was always under the risk of something happening.

No, no matter how much he thought about it, he could not figure out his brother's motives for joining this hunting expedition. In any case, the fact was that he had decided to help his captors, and he owed his present captivity and most probably his future death sentence to this collaboration.

The exile remained immersed in these thoughts during the two days following his kidnapping until one morning he had the feeling that they were being followed. He discovered it quite fortuitously.

His hands were tied to the saddle, and in an attempt to scratch his chin, he turned his head to the right to brush it against his shoulder. It was precisely at that moment that he looked back and made out a group of four men. Most likely they were merely travelers, but if he could get their attention...

Unfortunately for the exile, he was not the only one who noticed the horsemen drawing close. Alfonso had stopped the horse and dismounted to stretch his legs and rub his sore knee when he saw them. The uneasy expression reflected on his worn face left little doubt that he had also grasped the possibility of danger. Despite his limp, he quickly went over to Fernando.

"Take this," he said as he held out a dagger that he took from his belt. "If he asks for help or if he tries to escape, do not hesitate to run him through. Someone who opposes the truth does not deserve to live."

Then Alfonso addressed the brother.

"If someone in that group tries to free him, you and I will fire our pistols at them and finish off anyone still alive with the swords. Agreed?"

The brother pursed his lips and nodded.

"Then everything is set," said Alfonso. "Let's stay here."

Fernando freed the exile's tied hands from the saddle. Then he felt Fernando grab one of his feet and push him up, throwing him up and over the saddle. He felt a sharp pain as he crashed to the ground, and for a moment he feared the fall had dislocated his shoulder. He quickly realized, however, that he had received a bad blow, but nothing was broken or dislocated. He wasn't so sure, though, that he would have the same luck the next time Fernando decided to use that method to get him off the horse.

"If you say anything, I have this," he heard Fernando say as he struck him with the dagger Alfonso had given him. Then he pulled him to his feet by his shoulders.

"They can see that he is tied...," said Alfonso. "Fernando, remove the ties, but don't lose sight of him. At the first dubious move, skewer him like a pig."

At a hundred paces, the four riders could be seen in more detail. Their somber attire made it likely that they came from the same city in whose outskirts the exile had been captured.

The exile wasn't the only one who thought that. He could see that both Alfonso and his brother reached for the pistols that were hanging from their saddles. When the riders were only a dozen paces away, the exile noticed how Fernando took the dagger from the sheath and, with a cocky look, began cleaning his fingernails with it. The exile prayed to God that the riders would not make a single move that could be misinterpreted, because it was obvious the villain would take advantage of it to stab him.

The riders stopped short of reaching them. In polished, almost elegant French, the man in front asked if they had had a mishap or if they needed help. Speaking in terrible Latin, typical of an unlearned priest, Alfonso replied that they were only resting and did not need anything.

At that moment, the exile sneezed. It was a loud, violent sneeze that made him bend over double. He straightened up, shook his head, and apologized while everyone present responded with a pious invocation.

The travelers politely took their leave of the group and continued on their way, but neither Alfonso nor the brother took their hand off their pistols. In fact, they continued like that until the figures became black dots that were swallowed by the horizon. As soon as they disappeared from sight, Fernando tied the exile's hands again.

"What do you think?" Alfonso said to the brother.

"I don't think they have anything to do with us," he replied curtly. "This is a busy road and we will likely meet similar people in the coming days."

"Yes," Alfonso agreed, "you're probably right."

"What are you laughing at, heretic?" Fernando's harsh, rude voice made his brother and Alfonso look at the exile. But he was not laughing. On the contrary, his face showed a serious expression that could have even been one of worry.

"I don't see him laughing," said the brother.

"I swear he was laughing," Fernando insisted, pointing the dagger at the exile. "He knows something we don't."

"He," said the brother, "knows a whole lot of things you don't know and will never know in your lifetime."

Fernando didn't say anymore, but the way he narrowed his eyes showed that he was aware of the blow that had been dealt to his self-esteem. He shot a look of hatred at the exile, spat on the ground, thrust the dagger as if to stab him, and then sheathed and stuck it in his belt.

"They are long gone," said the brother. "Let's keep going."

The group started up again. Calmly, slowly, even cuatiously. Alfonso clenched his teeth from time to time when his knee troubled him; the brother wore an expression of grim mistrust; Fernando caressed the dagger, longing to use it.

The exile smiled.

CHAPTER 19

The only ambushes that have any guarantee of success are those that take full advantage of the element of surprise. An enemy that is surprised by its adversary loses precious moments before he realizes what is happening. Frequently, everything is decided in those moments, and it is not unusual for a small but bold and fast group to prevail over another stronger and more powerful one that has been distracted.

Both Alfonso and the brother were quite aware of that essential lesson in tactics. Both were also sure that Fernando, dimwitted as he was, would not react competently in such an event, so it was essential for them to keep their eyes open at all times. That was how they both spotted a small bridge several hundred paces away.

That tiny stone connection between the two banks of a stream was the perfect place for a trap. Anyone could intercept them from the other side of the stream and prevent them from passing. On top of that, a couple of rows of trees on both sides of the road made an ideal hiding place for a shooter. The brother gestured to Alfonso to move away. Alfonso spurred his horse and rode ahead a few paces. No, they wouldn't catch them unawares. Soon they reached the bridge.

Alfonso was about to cross over when a shot rang out. He turned and looked at the brother, but before they could exchange a word, a clear, calm voice came from some hidden point:

"Release the prisoner! Don't try anything because we are aiming at you."

Without a word, Alfonso dug his spurs into his mount, trying to get over the narrow bridge as the others followed. He didn't get very far. The exile could see a bullet enter his knee, precisely the one that was bothering him, leaving a hole that instantly oozed blood. He let out a wild howl of pain. Screaming in anguish from the bullet wound, Alfonso managed to get the pistol out of the saddle, but blind with pain and rattled because he couldn't see his opponent, he didn't know where to shoot. He had unwittingly become a target of any projectile with lethal intent.

"Get off your horse!" shouted the brother as he jumped off his own mount and hid behind the animal, using its body as cover. Almost totally protected by the noble beast, he began to move backward.

The exile thought that unless he was mistaken, his brother intended to protect himself under the bridge, as he himself had done weeks before when fleeing from his pursuers. There was no doubt that it would be easier for him to defend himself from that new position. It was then that he felt someone place his hands under the sole of his boot and push him up.

Once again the exile was thrown over the side of the saddle, but this time he did not fall to the ground, but against the side of the bridge. And he did not collapse to the ground. He quickly leaned his hands on the low stone wall, pushed himself to his feet, and started running. Suddenly he saw Fernando, who had unsheathed the dagger and was approaching him, clearly intent on killing him. For an instant the exile stopped. With his hands tied he couldn't defend himself against that beast who looked like a bull about to rush at him. Unless ... unless...

"Fernando, what are you going to spend the reward on? Wine? Because your wife is a drunk as everyone knows, and drinks..."

Fernando became enraged and stopped dead in his tracks. Then he gave a subhuman cry and charged the exile. The latter did not attempt to flee. When Fernando was a few steps from him, he crouched down and launched himself at him. He hit Fernando so hard on his Adam's apple that he was thrown back a full body length. Fernando put his hands to his neck and gurgled what sounded like curses, the dagger falling to the ground and sliding down the stones of the bridge.

The exile took advantage of Fernando's vulnerability and ran. He stepped on and over the young man's chest as he tried to reach the end of the bridge. He turned his head for a moment and could see Alfonso, his face red, pointing the pistol at him. He heard the gun go off and immediately the bullet whistled by his ear but didn't touch it. He looked back again and there was Fernando, about to stab him in the back.

The exile spun to the side but was unable to avoid the knife entirely. In fact, the dagger hit him on the shoulder and slid down the back of his arm to his wrist. The wound wasn't very deep but only one inch in the other direction would have been fatal.

The exile repeated the movement that had freed him from Fernando a few moments before. He tilted his head and this time launched it against Fernando's flabby, bulging abdomen. Letting out a groan, Fernando collapsed again, but this time he recovered instantly. In one movement he was up and leapt at the exile.

Once, twice, three times, the exile dodged Fernando's ruthless and hate-filled stabs.

"You dog, stand still!" Fernando screamed.

But the exile had no intention of making it easier for the young man to satisfy his murderous appetite. Although older than Fernando, he was also more agile and adroitly took advantage of his rival's dull clumsiness.

"If you don't get me, I don't know what your wife will drink...," he said.

"Aaaagh!" Fernando howled as he attempted another stab that missed like the previous ones. This time, the exile was able to move to one side and nimbly trip Fernando, throwing him against the stones of the bridge.

Quickly, he glanced at the other side of the bridge. Alfonso was falling from his saddle with an expression of excruciating pain on his face. His brother must have fired the pistol because now, sword in hand, he was preparing to continue the fight. Oh no! No! Why didn't he surrender?

That moment of distraction proved disastrous for the exile. Fernando dragged himself to him, grabbed the ankles of the man he hated, and pulled him to the ground. The exile only realized what happened when he felt Fernando's heavy body on top of him, holding down his arms with the weight of his knees.

"I'm not going to kill you yet, heretic dog, not yet," Fernando said before striking the exile's face with the hand that held the dagger.

It was a formidable blow, made more powerful by the weight of the dagger. The exile felt the entire inside of his skull burst with a wave of excruciating pain that spread from the wound on the top of his head to his chin and nose.

The following blows were no less painful. Years of envy for what he would never be, years of ingratitude for unmerited benefits, years of anger at having to ask for help, years of suffering caused by having to contemplate someone who was much better than he, all this he unloaded onto the exile's face. But the more he hit the more anger he felt. He did not feel less pain in his soul but more.

Finally, Fernando stopped for a moment. He was panting now, exhausted from the enormous effort, and he desperately needed to catch his breath. He took a deep breath, and as if handing down a sentence, he said:

"And now it ends."

He grasped the dagger with both hands and raised it high to plunge it into the neck of his victim.

"Blessed Virgin, help me!" shouted the young man with a triumphant shriek.

The exile closed his eyes and in his heart commended his soul to God. In an instant, he would find himself on the other side, he thought. However, instead of a dagger entering his body, he felt a weight fall on his chest, making it hard to breathe. He opened his eyes and realized that Fernando was lying motionless on top of him and that a hot, sticky liquid was seeping onto his chest. He immediately wondered if he was wounded, but then he understood.

His brother was standing before him, holding a bloody sword. Was he going to finish off what Fernando had not been able to accomplish? No. His brother, the one who for years had felt enmity towards him, the one who had accompanied Alfonso and Fernando, the one who had collaborated in his abduction.... this brother had just killed the vile resentful man who had been about to take him out of this world. His brother had saved his life.

The exile then saw men dressed all in black, some of whom were not entirely unfamiliar to him reach his brother and disarm him. In the background, a kneeling and howling Alfonso was held in shackles. Then he didn't see anything more.

CHAPTER 20

"They understood that you didn't leave of your own free will when you bowed your head and revealed the wound on your head."

The person who explained what had happened was the doctor friend who a few weeks before had welcomed him not as a poor refugee, but as a valued colleague in the art of healing.

"That was my intention," said the exile.

"Well, it certainly couldn't have gone better," he said with a warm smile. "They understood your message perfectly."

"I suppose they didn't try to free me then because..."

"For the simple reason that they feared the big fellow next to you would poke you full of holes. I have seen the corpse. Quite a brute ... but I don't get the impression that he liked to work too much."

"No, he didn't, in fact," the exile said with a smile. "To tell the truth, he was quite lazy."

"Well, now he is going to rest for all of eternity; although I'm afraid not exactly in a pleasant place."

A cloud of sorrow settled over the exile at the thought. It was true that Fernando had treated him despicably. It was also true that he had wanted to kill him and that only by the infinite mercy of God had he been prevented from perpetrating such a crime, but even so he did not harbor any rancor towards him.

After all, he had been the victim of a series of misfortunes that had accumulated throughout his life and fused into the blackest of envies. One could probably consider Fernando's death as an act of cosmic justice, but how many have deserved it as much or more than he did, and yet lived to a ripe old age?

"What is going to happen to them?" the exile asked with heaviness.

His companion in so many of his lost chess games took a deep breath before he answered.

"That fellow Alfonso will face severe punishment. Abducting a person and attempting to hand him over to the Holy Office to be put to death... yes, his punishment will not be light."

"What about my brother?" the exile interrupted him.

"Well ... there is no denying he accompanied them and that he collaborated in the kidnapping.... Even Alfonso insists that it was your brother who gave you the initial blow to the head..."

"Nobody in their right mind would believe a single word that comes out of Alfonso's mouth, nobody. He will only say what is in his interest even if it means harming the innocent. So then, what is going to happen to my brother?"

"If you..."

"If I what?"

"If you testify on behalf of your brother..."

"I will do that."

"Claiming what?"

"That from the very beginning his intention was to save me."

"You must admit, that is very difficult to believe..."

"Maybe, but I am following the evidence. He could have killed me countless times, and yet he prevented Fernando from doing so."

"Would you be willing to give that testimony before a judge?"

"Of course, and furthermore..."

"Furthermore?"

"In this city torture is not used to obtain confessions. No one will force him to deny my words."

"Thank God for that," acknowledged the doctor. "Yes, it is possible that your brother will be totally acquitted of any charges brought against him."

"Then everything is settled," the exile said, wanting nothing more than to conclude the matter.

"Yes," the doctor with the goatee agreed, "I suppose so."

The exile's friend paused, stroking his beard. It was obvious that he still had something to say. Finally, he broke the silence.

"The fact that you have managed to be saved has its advantages, but also its drawbacks."

"The advantages I can imagine," said the exile, "but what would be the drawbacks?"

"Before you arrived in this city there was a price put on your head."

"I had no idea."

"It wasn't much of a price."

"I'm not worth much," said the exile, unable to keep from smiling.

"Maybe, but be that as it may, the fact is that now the price has risen."

"Meaning..."

"Meaning you will have to be more cautious. You won't be able to leave the limits of the city. You should even try to be accompanied by someone when you walk out on the streets."

"I'll keep that in mind."

"No. You will not keep it in mind," corrected the doctor. "You will do it."

"All right," the exile conceded, "I will listen to you and obey. Do you have anything else to add?"

"I don't think so," the doctor answered with a smile.

The man with the goatee started to leave, but the exile held out his hand to stop him, though the gesture elicited a groan of pain.

"Wait, please. I'd like to ask you a couple of questions."

"Very well, but be brief. You need to rest."

"How did you notice that I had been abducted?"

"It was due to your punctuality. You are like the people of this city—you are never late for anything. One could almost set the clocks by watching you go by. When we saw that you did not come to your appointments, we concluded that something must have happened to you."

The exile's lips now parted in a wider, almost joyous smile. He knew that if he had been kidnapped in his country of origin, unquestionably it would have taken much longer, perhaps days, to suspect a mishap.

"I understand. Second question: how long will it take me to recover?"

"I am sure you are as or more capable than I am of responding to that question. You have some loose molars, though they are not damaged, and I imagine that your face and body will continue to hurt for a while. But really, you just have a lot of bruises. Two weeks, three at the most, and you will be attending to the sick as before."

"One last question."

"Another one?" said the doctor feigning impatience. "All right, go ahead."

"I know I won't be able to leave this city for a long time, maybe never ... but ... but..."

"Yes...?"

"Would it be possible for some people to come here to live with me?"

"How many people are you thinking of?"

"Three."

The doctor took a deep breath, ran his hand over his goatee again, and said:

"As I see it, you make more than enough to provide for them, which means they wouldn't be a burden on the city. That is essential, believe me, that they do not become a burden. But you ... you earn a very good living. So ... yes, I think you could tell them to come. And now, if you don't need anything else..."

"Yes, doctor, yes, there's just one more thing...," said the exile.

"Tell me."

"I want to thank you..."

"Oh dear God! That is not necessary," the doctor, raised his hands in an attempt to stop him.

"Yes, it is. You are not only an extraordinary doctor but you are also an exceptional colleague. Furthermore, you are a good Christian."

"Well..." the doctor tried again to stop the exile.

"There's no use denying it. It is true that you are not a clergyman, nor do you teach the Scriptures or serve from a pulpit, but the way in which you have put your work at the service of others, not for gold or for glory, but for the love of God and neighbor, is an example of what it means to be a Christian."

"If you are trying to embarrass me, you have succeeded, but I will not allow another word."

"The only thing I want is for you to know that I am grateful to you and that I will never forget what you have done for me."

"Do you need anything else?" the doctor asked with a trace of impatience in his voice.

"No, nothing more," replied the exile smiling again. "Go with God and may He bring you back soon."

"May it be so."

The doctor bowed his head slightly, turned, and left the room. The exile watched him leave and then turned his gaze to the window. He could see a section of the building across the way and a piece of clear sky. He tried to sit up, but the pain in his ribs dissuaded him from making any more movements.

Well, he told himself, the discomfort would last only a few weeks, and in reality, he could only thank God for everything that had happened in the previous months. He had saved his life over and over again and freed him from being taken to be burned in fires that were burning all over his home country. He had allowed him to reach a place where work was not a curse but a blessing, where the law was the same for everyone, where a judge could not also be the mayor and lawmaker, where education was part of daily life from childhood on, where science was appreciated, not despised, where no one was allowed to live at the expense of others, where those who could contribute something were warmly welcomed rather than attacked out of envy...

Not everything was perfect in that place, of course. Sickness, old age, and death still existed, and of course, humans demonstrated daily that the Fall was not just a theological concept, but ... but despite that, this new world was far superior to the one from which he had been forced to flee and where merely thinking differently could be reason enough to be reduced to ashes at the stake.

A new life had begun and in that new life, the exile would finally cease to be one.

AUTHOR'S COMMENTS

There is a common question for those of us who read novels. We want to know to what extent the facts described in their pages correspond to reality and to what extent they are the result of the author's imagination.

In the case of *The Exile*, the answer is very simple. First, all the characters who appear in these chapters are imaginary except for Juan Díaz, a Spanish Protestant who was assassinated, thanks to his brother who could not bear the existence of a heretic in the family.

However, despite the imaginary character of all the other participants in the story, the world it describes corresponds closely to the reality of the time.

It would be too long and tedious to explain every detail in this regard, but a few can be pointed out by way of example. An expert on sixteenth-century history will recognize that in the exile's conversation with the mayor and the priest, I quote verbatim from Alfonso de Valdés. Also, the decree defended by Alfonso that prohibited Spaniards from studying at foreign universities to prevent them from accepting heretical positions was enacted by Philip II in November of 1559. And beginning with

Geneva in 1556, compulsory and free schools were introduced into European territories that joined the Reformation, as part of the program of reform. Finally, the view of work was radically different in the Europe of the Counter-Reformation versus the Europe of the Reformation.

All these details and others that are reflected in this book are strictly historical.

However, *The Exile* is not only an account of the time of the Reformation and the Counter-Reformation ... although it is that. The fact is, it constitutes a description of how different societies define and shape not only the present but also the future based on the values they embrace. These values make them strong or quite weak when dealing with crises and also put them on the path to either a prosperous future or a repetition of disasters already suffered in the past.

Much in the previous pages has a paradigmatic character that transcends time and place. It is not an accident that the exile is exactly that, an exile, and like so many before or after him, he has no name in the vast ocean of history.

The same could be said of brothers and doctors, rogues and clergymen, friends and loved ones, children and judges. However, despite their anonymity, each and every one of them is affected by the social mores surrounding them.

There is a difference in societies where education is important, where there is a true separation of powers, where science is promoted, where work is not considered a disgrace, but a form of service to others, and those where the talented are attacked rather than welcomed for making positive contributions to the whole of society.

Therefore, *The Exile* is a work of fiction, but it addresses real and, above all, transcendental questions for societies and people, people whose names will never appear in books as is the case with the protagonist and others in this novel.

But not for this reason have they stopped making contributions, often mean and reprehensible, like those of Fernando and Alfonso, but also beautiful and positive like those of the exile's neighbor, the doctor with the goatee, and Marguerite.

César Vidal

(Miami, April of 2020, in the midst of the coronavirus crisis)